Marzipan and Murder

A BITE-SIZED BAKERY COZY MYSTERY BOOK 2

ROSIE A. POINT

Cover by Fantasy Fig Designs

You're invited!

Hi there, reader!

I'd like to formally invite you to join my awesome community of readers. We love to chat about cozy mysteries, cooking, and pets.

It's super fun because I get to share chapters from yet-to-be-released books, fun recipes, pictures, and do giveaways with the people who enjoy my stories the most.

So whether you're a new reader or you've been enjoying my stories for a while, you can catch up with other like-minded readers, and get lots of cool content by visiting my website at *www.rosiepointbooks.com* and signing up for my mailing list.

Or simply search for me on *www.bookbub.com* and follow me there.

I look forward to getting to know you better.

Let's get into the story!

Yours,
Rosie

One

"I KNOW WHO YOU ARE," SAID THE WOMAN, HER gray hair piled in ringlets atop her head. She paused, clutching a few dollars in her fist. "You're the one who solved Owen's murder."

It was hardly the opener to a conversation I would've expected from one of my customers. But I'd had plenty of questions and chats like it in the weeks Bee and I had spent in Carmel Springs, Maine, baking up a storm and serving people out of the side of my candy-striped food truck.

The small town had already surprised me. And not just with its sumptuous lobster rolls.

"I'm Ruby." I brushed my palms off on my cutesy striped apron and presented a hand through the side window of the truck. "Ruby Holmes."

"Of the Sherlock variety?" The woman showed me a

white-toothed grin. She was chubby around the cheeks and waist and wore a long, flowery coat over a cream blouse.

"Not quite," I replied. "But it's nice to meet you, um…"

"Oh, how rude of me. Sorry," she said, "I'm Mary-Lynn. Mary-Lynn Miller, but everyone calls me Millie, and you're welcome to as well." She took a step back, her boots gritting on the asphalt, and smiled at the truck. "A few of the ladies in my knitting circle were gossiping about your truck the other day, and I had to come down and see what the fuss was about. I hope you don't mind."

Bee rose from where she'd been crouching, keeping an eye on this week's treat—vanilla-caramel cupcakes. We planned on injecting them with a delicious caramel filling once they were cool and topping them with a matching frosting.

"Oh!" Millie gave a sharp cry. "I didn't see you there."

"That's because I didn't want you to," Bee replied evenly.

"This is Bee, by the way."

"Nice to meet you, Bee-by-the-way," Millie said. "You know, I'm somewhat of a baker myself."

"Is that why you've come to the truck?" I asked, trying not to sound too desperate.

The sun was bright, the ocean choppy, the wind cold,

and it was a perfect day for a baked treat and a cup of hot coffee, but the food truck hadn't been doing that well lately. Bee and I had discussed packing up and moving on to the next town.

After the murder the week before, people's enthusiasm for our treats—cupcakes, cookies, donuts, and more—had dwindled sufficiently. I theorized that was because the detective in town had taken it upon himself to confiscate our truck and blame me for the murder.

Even though we'd helped put the real murderer behind bars, the opinion that I had been involved somehow had remained.

Millie didn't answer my question but disappeared around the side of the truck.

"And I thought I was strange," Bee whispered.

At sixty-plus-years-old, single, and tight-lipped about her mysterious past, my partner in baking was the epitome of different. And I liked that. I wasn't normal either— having a keen eye and a difficult past did that to a lady.

Millie reappeared, patting her hair, icy blue eyes darting from left to right. "It's lovely," she said. "Not at all what the ladies said it would be."

"What did they say it would be?" Oh heavens, did I want to know what the local gossip crew thought about the food truck? Would it break my heart and speed my exit from this small town and into the next one? I hadn't felt this out-of-place before and, given my history, that said a lot.

"Hmm, well." Millie wriggled her nose. "That it had been trashed and was dilapidated. And that the food here was stale."

"Oh." My shoulders drooped. It was no wonder our customer base had dropped off the side of a cliff. Good heavens, it was already past ten and Millie was our first customer of the morning.

On our first day on the truck, we'd been run ragged with customers. The comparison was stark and, frankly, gut-wrenching. I loved the atmosphere in the town, the scent of the ocean, and the smiles of the locals, even if they weren't always directed at us, but if business didn't pick up soon, we'd have no choice but to leave.

"Don't worry about them, dear," Millie said, flapping her hands at me. "They don't have inquiring or particularly sharp minds. But I do."

"Is that so?" Bee brought the cupcakes from the oven and delivered them to the countertop.

"Why, I'm here, aren't I?" Millie turned in a circle, waving her arms over herself, flamboyantly. "Here to save the day."

"Save the day?" I didn't dare hope.

"I'm the editor of the local newspaper," Millie said. "I have some degree of control over what's published and when. I'll get one of the food critics to come down and have a taste of your treats. The proof is in the pudding."

"Assuming they don't drop dead, that's a great idea."

I nudged Bee, but she only gave another of her gap-toothed smiles.

"She's kidding," I said. "It was a reference to—"

Again, Millie flapped her hands. "Oh, I know. I know." She laughed, her eyes sparkling. "I thought, perhaps, I could—"

A yell rang out.

We all leaned forward, tracking the source of the cry.

Two women stormed up the street toward us. As they drew closer to the truck, their voices drifted over. One of the women wore her platinum blonde hair long.

It was Honey Wilson, the newest guest at the Oceanside Guesthouse, Sam's quaint place that had been our impromptu home for the past few weeks. Honey was loud, girly, and obnoxious. A strange combination for a woman so small.

She stopped next to one of the benches that overlooked the sandy beach below, stomping a foot and glaring at the lady who accompanied her. Tall, redheaded, and wearing a pantsuit and a severe frown, she scowled at Honey.

"—think I'm going to do that, you're crazy," Honey

said. "I'm telling you, I'm not going to sacrifice my special day for your idiot ideas."

"Oof," Millie said, leaning one arm on the truck's counter as she watched the blowout.

"Who's the redhead?" Bee asked. "Haven't seen her around."

"No idea," Millie replied. "She must be from out of town."

"How do you figure that?"

"I know everyone and everything that happens in Carmel Springs." Millie's confidence shone through the words. "If she was a local, I'd already have her complete history on file."

I lifted my finger to my lips.

The argument had reached its peak. "—can't help you if you won't let me, Ms. Wilson."

"Then I won't let you."

"You can't seriously mean that. I came all the way from LA for this."

"Enough." Honey put up a hand, rolling her head at the other woman and clicking her fingers. "I'm done. And so are you." She turned on her stiletto heel and pranced up the street, her high ponytail swinging back and forth in a very "Marcia, Marcia, Marcia" fashion.

The redhead whispered something under her breath,

her lips peeling back in a rictus, then marched away in the opposite direction.

"Well, that was interesting," Millie said. "And it's upped my appetite too. May I have the, let's see, a vanilla-caramel cupcake?"

"Absolutely," I said, true joy spinning through my stomach. A new customer and maybe even a new friend. It was a good start to the day, arguments aside.

Two

"WHAT DO YOU THINK WE SHOULD DO, BEE?" I asked as we took our seats at the table in the Oceanside Guesthouse's warm open plan dining area. Once again, Sam had started a fire behind the grate, and logs crackled and popped nearby.

"What do you mean?" Bee asked.

"Oh, you know, the truck. Maybe you were right last week. We should have left after the investigation ended."

The living room was empty but would soon fill with people coming to enjoy their breakfasts. Sam was such a whiz when it came to cooking. She'd taken to preparing three meals a day, including snacks for guests, and we were there for almost every one of them.

How could we resist?

"I don't know," Bee said.

"You don't? You were the one who suggested it."

"Yes, I was." Bee scanned the living room, her hazel eyes bright. "But now that we've been here for a while, I'm not as sure. From a business perspective, it would be better to move on, but that would be like giving up."

That didn't help much. But I trusted Bee to be blunt about her feelings.

"Maybe we should stay for a few days?"

"Maybe," Bee said. "Let's see if that Millie woman comes back today. We could talk to her about the rumors she's heard, perhaps even get her to publish a piece in the local newspaper about the truck?"

"I'm not sure I have the funds to pay for a sponsored message. We haven't exactly been flush with customers the past—"

The swinging doors to the kitchen opened, and Sam, the owner, emerged. She smiled and came over. "Good morning," she sang. "How did you sleep?"

"Fantastic, as usual, Sam, thank you," I replied.

"Your guesthouse is so comfortable," Bee added. "How could we not be well-rested after a night on feather pillows?"

"Have you been using your fireplaces?" Sam asked. "It's been cold the past few evenings."

"I did," Bee said. "I was toasty warm all night."

Samantha was such a sweetheart, and she was another

reason I'd be sad to leave Carmel Springs when we decided to go. That and her adorable cat, Trouble, who'd taken a liking to me. He was stretched out on the rug a few feet back from the fireplace, his eyes half-open as he dozed, purring loudly.

"What's on the menu for breakfast today?" I asked, checking that we were on time.

"I've got fried eggs and bacon, eggs Benedict, or omelets for you to choose from. I'll also be serving a fruit parfait with fresh yogurt and granola. And there will be oatmeal if you'd like to skip out on any of the above."

"Wow." My mouth watered. "That sounds amazing."

"I can't wait to taste it."

"We'll just wait for the other guests to come down, shall we?" Sam wrung her hands. She was always concerned about whether we were settled or not. Partly, I figured, because she had inherited this little guesthouse from her grandmother. And she was a nice person. One could never put a price on kindness and respect.

We waited for the other guests to arrive.

Sam had a habit of encouraging people to talk over breakfast. On Sundays, she would push all the square tables in the dining area together, so we'd be forced to eat and talk. Bee wasn't the biggest fan of that kind of thing, but I liked it. The different personalities intrigued me.

A clatter of footsteps on the wooden staircase

announced the arrival of some of the others. And a good thing too. I was about ready to eat my placemat.

A young woman entered, and I did a double-take. It was Honey, the blonde we'd witnessed in an argument in front of the truck the day before. She was in tears, wiping a finger beneath either eye as she took her place on the far side of the table.

I turned in my seat, searching for her fiancé, William, but he hadn't come down yet. All in all, there were currently six guests, including Bee and me. Where were the others?

Honey sniffled and hiccupped.

"Are you all right?" I asked, scooching my chair out.

Honey's bottom lip quivered.

"Oh dear," Sam whispered. "Oh dear. Oh no. What's the matter? Was it the cocoa? Did Mirabelle forget to refill your sugar pot?" The fact that she thought a sugar pot was a crying matter was both sweet and naïve.

Honey shook her head. "I just... I..." She dissolved into a puddle of tears.

Bee shifted, clearing her throat. "Well. That's uncomfortable."

"Let me handle this," I whispered to my friend.

"Rather you than me." Bee didn't trust easily. But she didn't panic either when serious things happened. I liked to think that my friend's strengths filled in the spots occupied by my shortcomings and vice versa.

I joined Honey and placed a hand on her forearm. "Are you all right?"

"Of course I'm not all right," Honey said. "Everything is an utter disaster. I'm smudging my makeup, William hasn't even hugged me yet this morning, and I don't have anyone to cater my wedding."

"Oh, that's—"

"My wedding planner was useless, so I had to fire her, and why I had to have my wedding in such a disgusting, pitiful small town is beyond me. This is not fair. It's not fair!"

I took a breath. *Disgusting small town?* That was hardly how I would describe Carmel Springs. Sure, I hadn't had the best experiences here, but it wasn't disgusting. It was quaint, and most of the people were lovely.

It seemed that Honey was either expecting too much or something else entirely. She struck me as the type who wanted a ceremony fit for a princess.

"I'm sorry," I said, withdrawing my hand from her arm.

"There's nothing for *you* to be sorry about," she snapped, clicking her manicured nails together. "It wasn't you who chose this place to—" Her eyes widened, and it was shocking—the smudged dark eye shadow made her look like a stunned raccoon. "Wait a second! I know who you are."

"Oh?" I glanced at Bee, who shook her head. "You do?"

"You're the woman who owns that silly little food truck."

"Uh."

"You cook! You bake! You can cater my wedding!"

"Oh boy," Bee said.

"I don't know if I'm the best person for that," I said, carefully. "We only do desserts."

"That's fine! I need a series of cupcakes for the wedding. I want a cupcake tower instead of a cake. You can do that, right? I mean, it's simple enough for you to handle. I know you're not gourmet or anything..."

"We specialize in gourmet cupcakes." I lifted my chin.

"Perfect. You'll do it then. Don't worry, I'll pay you well. Above your rate," Honey said. "Name the price and it's yours, just please, please help me. The wedding is next week."

"That's awfully short notice," I said.

"Please?"

Business *had* been slow, and helping Honey might give us more credibility in town. From what I'd heard, the groom had a lot of family in Carmel Springs. If we did pull this off, we might benefit from more than the price Honey was willing to meet.

Bee nodded at me.

"All right," I said. "We'll do it."

"Oh, wonderful!" Honey squealed and clapped her hands. "Wonderful."

"What's going on?" William, her fiancé, had appeared at the foot of the stairs. The other two guests stood behind him. His twin brother, Richard, looked almost exactly like William, from the dark hair to the eyes and strong, sharp nose. He scowled at Honey.

Jessie, her maid of honor, who might have been a carbon copy of Honey except for the fact that she wore her hair short and brown, rushed to the bride's side. "What's wrong? You look like you've been crying."

"Did I ruin my makeup?" Honey wailed and dove for the compact in her purse.

I returned to my seat next to Bee.

"Looks like it's going to be an interesting day," Bee whispered.

"At least we'll get paid." A knot of tension tightened in my belly. Who knew what this week would bring?

Three

AFTER THE BREAKFAST—FRUIT PARFAIT AND EGGS Benedict for me—Bee and I retired to our bedrooms to discuss what had happened. We'd been planning on attending the local museum and finding out more about the history in Carmel Springs, but the prospect of a new job took precedence.

"What do you think?" I shut my bedroom door. "Did I make the right decision?"

"Don't be so unsure of yourself, Ruby," Bee said, in a tone that was half-cold and half-motherly. "Really, you're almost forty years old. You shouldn't doubt yourself as much as you do."

"You're right." And she was, but I couldn't help it. I'd spent years in a relationship with a man who had broken me down. The only time I'd felt confident was when I'd been interviewing people for articles or writing stories for the paper. Apparently, decisions related to my business fell under the "insecurity" tag.

I'd have to get over it.

"Interesting, though," Bee said, walking to the coffee station in the corner of the room. She made a mean pot of Joe.

I sat down and kicked off my shoes, tucking my feet underneath me in the armchair. "What is? The wedding?"

"Everything about it. Honey and her fiancé included." Bee doled out coffee grounds into the receptacle. "Don't you find it strange that she didn't cry to him instead of coming downstairs and weeping by herself at the breakfast table?"

"Hmm."

"She could have spoken to that friend of hers, Jessie, but she didn't. Why do you think that was?"

"Perhaps an attention-seeking move?" I asked. "Maybe she wanted everyone to feel sorry for her."

"Valid point. It's odd, though. A woman like that surely gets more than enough attention." Bee gestured with a spoon. "Look at her, for heaven's sake. She looks as if she's stepped off the cover of a magazine."

I paused, biting on the inside of my cheek. I had learned to gossip at the paper—it was necessary to ask awkward questions and have whispered conversations to find the truth—but I'd tried to rid myself of the habit once I'd quit and bought the food truck.

So much for that idea. "Do you remember the day they first arrived in Carmel Springs?"

"Vividly," Bee said. "Honey threw a fit over having to get married in William's hometown. He carried the bags into the guesthouse after her like a puppy dog."

"Harsh."

"And then they had a rip-roaring argument later that night. I could barely sleep," Bee said, as she clicked on the machine, allowing the grounds to steep and the vitality-giving liquid to burble out into the glass pot below.

"Well, let's hope they've resolved their issues. They seemed fine at breakfast. You saw how they were whispering and cuddling over their shared omelet."

"Most off-putting," Bee said.

"This wedding might be what puts us back on the map in town. I wanted our first venture out on our food truck to be successful. And we can't leave before that new supply of boxes gets to the post office here."

Bee gave me a warm smile. "It will work out, Ruby. Don't you worry."

Footsteps thumped down the hall outside and stopped outside my bedroom door. A curt knock came next.

Bee and I stiffened.

It was probably just one of the guests. Albeit one who

walked like they'd been cursed with giant feet. The murder and the ensuing investigation from the mean detective last week had us on edge. It was silly. Carmel Springs was safe.

I answered the door and found Honey tapping her fingernails on the jamb. "There you are," she said. "We haven't finished talking about the wedding." She forced her way into the room without invitation.

"Come on in," Bee said.

Honey ignored her. "So." She folded her arms. "As I said, I want them to be wedding cupcakes. Like, a whole tiered, layered thing of cupcakes. Get it?"

"Sure," I said.

"Why aren't you taking notes?" Honey demanded. "I don't work with amateurs. I want notes taken so you don't get it wrong."

"Surely, an amateur would get it wrong with or without notes."

This time, Honey shot Bee a scathing look.

I brought my phone out and opened up my Notes app. I typed out her first request—or rather, command—then waited for the next one.

"Good. That's better. The last woman who worked for me was an incompetent fool." She smacked her lips. "Do you know anything about organizing weddings?"

"No," I said quickly. "Just baking." And even that was crossing a line. Bee was the baker. I was the truck driver and business owner. But in the past two weeks, I'd picked up a few tricks from my partner. I could whip up a mean miniature banana bread.

"Oh." Her lips turned down at the corners. "I want to taste your stuff first before I hire you. I've already got the event prepared. We're holding the wedding at the town hall." If anything, her expression grew more disdainful. "And you can use their kitchen to prepare the cupcakes when I do hire you."

"All right," I noted that down for posterity.

"I'm going to be busy scouting a new organizer for the wedding," Honey continued, none of her weepiness present anymore. "I want you to prepare a set of sample cupcakes and drop them off at the town hall by tomorrow morning. You can come by in the afternoon, and I'll tell you my verdict. Do you understand?"

"Sure," I said slowly.

"But the cupcakes will cost you," Bee put in. "The testers. Ingredients don't come cheap."

Honey glared at Bee.

My cheeks grew warm. Once again, Bee had stepped in where I might not have. She was always looking out for our best interests.

"Fine." Honey waved a hand. "I'll pay you for the test cupcakes. But they had better be good. They had better be worth my time. Now, I'll expect that delivery there by nine, as I'll be at the town hall an hour after. You're to come back at 2:00 p.m. No sooner. No later. Understood?"

"Sure," I said.

"Good." She swept from the room and nearly tripped over Trouble in the hall. "Stupid cat!"

Trouble darted toward us, and I lifted him into my arms, stroking his soft calico fur. Before I could say anything about her insult, Honey had marched off, her stilettos heavy on the wooden boards.

"She's delightful," Bee said.

"A real treat," I agreed.

"Are you sure you want to do this?"

Trouble purred and rubbed the side of his kitty face against my hand. "Yeah," I said, "I'm sure. This will give me a chance to make my famous marzipan frosting."

"Famous?"

"OK, not famous. But it's the frosting that inspired my love for baking. It was my grandmother's special recipe, and it's probably the only thing I can make that tastes delicious, rather than just OK."

Bee poured us our coffees, and I returned to my comfy, flower-patterned armchair with Trouble. He purred and clawed my hand when I rubbed his belly, clearly in the mood for play, but all I could think about was the wedding, cupcakes, and Honey Wilson's foul attitude.

Four

"WHAT A BEAUTIFUL DAY." WE STOOD ON THE wooden overlook near the beach. The waves weren't as choppy today, and the view of the ocean was what had kept me in Carmel Springs. That and the seafood.

My belly rumbled at the thought.

"Hungry?" Bee asked.

"You can say that again. Do you think we have time to grab lunch before we head over to the town hall?" I checked my watch. "Ugh, no we don't. It's already a quarter to, and she wants us there at 2:00 p.m. on the dot."

"Bit of a megalomaniac if you ask me," Bee said. "What with the hair and the heels and the commands. She would fit in well in the army."

"Even with the hair and the heels?"

"All right, a fashionable army. She could have a show like Joan Rivers did. Remember her?"

"I never watched those shows," I said. "But I'm sure you're right. Honey is very stylish."

"At least she's got *that* going for her."

"Bee."

"It's difficult for me to be polite when other people aren't," Bee said.

"Let's get going." I'd have to wait until after our meeting with Honey to grab a bite. We'd planned on checking out more of the local restaurants, since the Lobster Shack was closed until further notice. Murder was never good for business, as I'd come to discover.

Then again, that was kind of a no-brainer. *Is that a horrible pun I just made? Ugh.*

"I would've liked to go somewhere for lunch," Bee said, as we turned off the long beach road and started toward the center of town, passing quaint stores with people both inside and out. A few of them smiled and nodded or greeted us as we passed.

It was a nice change from the outright suspicion the week before. "Samantha will have a snack for us when we get back. And we shouldn't have taken the day off because of the cupcakes."

"Unfortunately, I don't think it made much of a difference," Bee said. "I doubt anyone stopped by at our usual spot overlooking the beach. At least not in search of our cakes."

"But the wedding will change that," I said.

"Yoo-hoo!" The call came from the butcher shop across the street. Both Bee and I watched as Millie, the rotund and friendly editor of the paper hurried toward us, flapping a hand in greeting. "There you are. I went down to the beachfront today, but your truck wasn't there."

"So someone did miss us," I said, brightening.

"Apart from business being slower than a frozen lobster," Bee noted.

"But we did just get an offer to cater a wedding. We're about to find out if we got the job."

Millie pursed her lips. "Don't tell me. It's the Wilson-Hall wedding?"

"Yeah. Why?"

"I heard Ms. Wilson is a real pain in the places the sun don't shine," Millie said. "But then, that's none of my business, now is it? I have good news."

"You do?" I was in desperate need of some.

"I've gotten one of the food critics at the paper to agree to taste your food and write up a review. How the review pans out will be up to you ladies, of course."

"Wow, that's fantastic!"

"Thanks," Bee said and gave the woman one of her

warmer smiles. "That's really appreciated. We could use all the help we can get now."

Just the fact that we were in conversation with Millie seemed to change our attitudes. As we went our separate ways, a few of the locals waved or stopped to chat with us. Millie's acceptance went a long way. Perhaps we had made a powerful ally.

We reached the town hall at 2:05 p.m. I despised tardiness, and the fact that we were late for a meeting with the bridezilla gave me waves of tummy nerves.

We entered the building and found the main hall empty. Chairs were set up facing a stage and a podium, and the place smelled of salt and wood polish, like the years of use in a coastal town had sunk into the furniture. I had trouble picturing how it would look decorated, and I'd thought the same when we'd delivered the cupcakes this morning.

"Where is she?" Bee checked her watch. "I might be the kettle here, but she's late."

"I wouldn't say that too loudly if I were you. I doubt Honey would take kindly to being called a pot."

"You really think she'd put the saying together?" Bee asked.

I pinched her on the elbow for her meanness, and she swatted me on the arm, grinning.

"But seriously," she said. "Where is she?"

"Maybe in the kitchen? That's where we had to drop off the cupcakes." I trooped across the hall and toward the shut kitchen door. The place didn't exactly have catering facilities, but the kitchen was big enough to prepare a few cakes, though we'd need to bring our own equipment on the wedding day.

I opened the door and stepped inside. It took a moment to register the scene in front of me, but when it clicked—

I let out a squeal and stumbled back, Bee catching me as I stepped on her toes. "Ouch! What? What is it?"

A body lay on the floor in the middle of the kitchen. A woman, with stiletto heels on, and... Oh, no.

"It's her. It's Honey," Bee whispered. "What's that on her face?"

A white cloth appeared to be stuck to her face. I approached, placing one foot carefully in front of the other. She definitely wasn't breathing, and the "cloth" was none other than marzipan. My marzipan. From my marzipan cupcakes.

"Bee," I said. "I think it's time we call 911."

Five

"ASPHYXIATION." DETECTIVE JONES GRABBED one of the chairs in the town hall. He spun it around on the spot then straddled it, his meaty, hairy arms balanced on its top rail.

"That's terrible," I whispered. The beginnings of nausea roiled in my belly. I'd never been good with anything regarding corpses or blood or murder. But then, who was?

Bee, apparently. My friend had taken charge the minute, "Call 911" had left my mouth. She'd effectively cordoned off the area, using a roll of kitchen towel, and had taken several pictures of the body on her phone, as well as of the cupcakes and all possible exits and entrances to the kitchen.

I had a hunch my friend wanted to take matters into her own hands. I was too nauseated to be curious just yet.

"Terrible," the detective said, bringing my focus back to his scowl. "Terrible that you were here in the first place."

Not this again. "Look, I've just witnessed a... Well, not a murder, but I've walked in on another dead body. I'm not in the mood to mince words, detective. Why don't you tell me what you need from me?"

"A confession," Jones replied.

"Excuse me?"

"Save us all some time and tell the truth. You killed her, didn't you?"

"I most definitely did not." Outrage swam through me. How dare he accuse me when he had no evidence? Sure, I happened to have been at the scene of the crime, and it was my special marzipan that had been plastered over her face, but—

"Your marzipan killed her."

"Excuse me, but my marzipan is soft and delicious. I don't know what you're—"

Detective Jones rolled his eyes. "No, she *actually* choked on it. The marzipan was the murder weapon."

"Oh. Oh no." Now, the outrage was gone, and I was just plain dizzy. How could this have happened? "This can't be happening."

"Because you've been caught?"

"What? No! Detective, this line of questioning is inappropriate. Bee and I came out here to meet with Honey about the cupcakes we'd be catering for her wedding."

"Let me guess. She told you she didn't like the cupcakes, and you two decided to take matters into your own hands. Kill her for it."

I'd started wondering if the detective had been dropped on his head as a child. "Listen, detective," I said, my tone stiffening now that some of the panic had dissipated. "Bee and I found a dead body, nothing more and nothing less. Why don't you get your forensic people to find out when the murder occurred? Bee and I were out on the street in full view of everyone five minutes before we found the body. There's no way we could have done this."

Jones glared at me. "That doesn't mean anything. You might have murdered her in the morning and come back in the afternoon to establish an alibi."

I let out a frustrated grunt.

"What's going on?" Bee marched toward us. "Is Serpico giving you trouble?"

"He's convinced that we committed the murder."

Jones's lips drew into a thin line at the sight of my baking partner. The pair didn't like each other. The attitude had been established during his last investigation because Bee was defensive of the food truck and of me as her friend.

"I'm taking Miss Holmes's statement. I'll need you to proceed to one of the seats over there and speak with Detective Martin."

Another detective had appeared, indeed, and walked over. He was the opposite of Jones in every way—smiling, tall, handsome, and young. "Ma'am? Could I speak to you for a second?" *And he's polite too.*

I cleared my throat.

Poor Honey—all right, so she wasn't "poor" so to speak—had been murdered, and it seemed as if someone had tried to frame the truck again. Or maybe, they'd been in such a rage they'd used whatever was closest to them to finish the job.

Bee and the handsome detective walked off and sat down out of earshot, Bee casting glances our way, her eyes narrowed to slits.

"I'm going to take your statement," Jones said, removing a pen from his pocket. "Need I remind you, *ma'am*, that lying in an official statement to the police is perjury and punishable by law."

"You don't need to remind me of anything." I folded my arms.

The statement-taking went relatively quickly, but Jones kept stalling as if he wanted to squeeze more from me or get me to say something to help his case. I'd always been of the opinion that police served and protected, and solved crimes obviously, but Jones soured that impression.

After the grueling interview, I stepped out onto the sidewalk and found the sun dipping toward the horizon.

"It's that late already?" Bee asked.

Several police cruisers were parked in front of the building, and an ambulance sat alongside them. Forensic technicians had pulled up outside and piled out of their vehicle, making for the front of the building in their funny white suits that crinkled as they walked.

"Oh boy," I said. "Here we go again."

Bee nodded and looped her arm through mine. We started up the sidewalk away from the noise. Most of the store owners in the street stood around, gossiping behind their hands and studying the town hall. A few of them pointed at us.

I'd been sure that things were about to get better for the food truck, but Honey's death definitely changed things.

"What are we going to do?"

"Go back to the guesthouse and rest," Bee said.

"Rest?"

"Rest being a euphemism."

"For what? Death?"

Bee managed a short, sharp laugh under her breath. "Investigating it. I took those pictures, remember? There's got to be something we can use to figure out who did this."

So there it was. Bee was determined to solve the mystery, even though it wasn't our business. Then again, if we didn't, Jones might use it as an excuse to blame us for it. "Do you think we'll be able to figure it out? From what we've seen so far, it's not like Honey was the most popular person around."

"Understatement of the year," Bee said, as we turned a corner and were met with another crowd of people heading toward the commotion.

We were bumped several times, but no one stopped or paid us any attention, which suited me fine. The less notice we garnered, the better it would be for the food truck. If Jones decided to confiscate it again... But, no, he couldn't do that. After all, we'd used Samantha's kitchen to make the cupcakes.

"Hmm."

"What?" Bee asked.

"I wonder if Samantha would know anything useful," I said. "She knows when the guests arrived and how long they're staying, and she's been in contact with them more than we have. We should talk to her about this."

"Now, there's a good idea." Bee shot me an approving grin. "We'll make a baker-sleuth out of you yet."

"I don't remember opting in to the 'sleuth' title."

"With a last name like Holmes, how could you not be a sleuth?"

Sleuth or not, I had to ensure this didn't affect the food truck. Jones wouldn't want us to leave town until this murder was solved. Though his version of "solved" likely involved us behind bars and him with less on his plate.

Not on my watch.

Six

THE OCEANSIDE GUESTHOUSE WAS SITUATED right on the beach, with a back porch that opened out on a gorgeous view of the sand below and the long trail that led down toward it. Bee and I positioned ourselves in wicker armchairs opposite each other, keeping our eye on the sliding glass doors that led into the living room.

No one was home.

Samantha had given all the guests keys for their rooms and the house itself, in case she had to run out for ingredients or anything else. And it seemed she'd chosen now to do that. Not exactly to plan with what we'd wanted to do —squeeze her for information.

"Where do you think she went?" I asked, tugging on my fingers.

"You must relax, Ruby," Bee said. "You're going to give yourself a hernia at this rate."

"Aren't hernias from lifting heavy objects?"

"True. A hernia is when the bowel pops out of the—"

"Nope!" I put up both palms. "That's more than enough information, thank you. If I want to know more, I'll search online."

Bee chuckled. "It's not that bad. Not as bad as death by marzipan."

"Ugh." I shook my head. "I don't understand how that's possible. You and I both know my marzipan is soft and delicious. And we covered those cupcakes so the coating wouldn't go hard."

"But really, they wouldn't have to be rock hard to choke a person. All it would take is a little force." Bee made a gesture with her arms and hands that I didn't care to examine too closely. "Just like that, and then that, and—"

The sliding door opened, and one of the guests, the brother of the groom, Richard, exited onto the porch. At least, I thought it was Richard. They were twins, and it was difficult to distinguish between them. This brother had a mole to the right of his mouth like Cindy Crawford. Except male.

He bobbed his head to us then stomped down the steps and took the long path to the sand, tucking his hands into the pockets of his chino pants. He'd rolled them up at the bottom but wore a pair of sneakers.

"Who wears closed shoes on the beach?" Bee whispered.

"That guy."

"I mean, really. What's the point of going to the beach if you're not going to wiggle your toes in the sand?"

"It's cold," I said, drawing my coat tighter around myself. "Maybe he doesn't want his toes frozen off by the wind."

"Or maybe he's up to something," Bee whispered. "The groom's brother, leaving the guesthouse? What if he's trying to run? He didn't look upset if you ask me."

"He might not know yet."

"Everyone knows. This is a small town." Bee scratched under her chin. "I don't like it, and I don't trust it."

"Don't trust what?" Sam stepped through the sliding door that Richard had left open. She wore a thick coat and a pair of woolen gloves. She stripped off the gloves, her cheeks a rosy pink.

"Oh nothing," Bee said, quickly. "Just idle chatter. I suppose you've heard?"

"About Honey?" Sam asked. "I was in the fruit aisle at the General Store when I found out. It was chaos."

"Why?" I shifted in my seat.

"It was announced over the loudspeaker. Old Man

Lester has never had a strong grasp on the meaning of the word tact. He announces everything over the loudspeaker in the store, from specials on ground beef to the untimely passing of Mrs. Rose's pet parakeet."

"And he did the same about Honey?"

"Yes. Poor Mrs. Crindle passed out on the grapefruits and caused a produce avalanche. They're still cleaning it."

Bee pulled a face. "Thank heavens she wasn't near the lobster tank."

Sam lowered herself onto the swinging seat, and Trouble *purred* his way onto the porch and leaped into her lap. She stroked his ears and turned her head toward the ocean. "What terrible news. I can't believe it."

"Can't you?" Bee asked.

Sam frowned.

"She means, um, that Honey was, well... What's the delicate way to put this?" I couldn't find it, whatever it was.

"Honey was mean and argumentative," Bee said.

Sam's cheeks grew even pinker. "I hate to speak ill of the dead, particularly so soon after *it* happened, but I can't say you're wrong. She was terrible to me when she first arrived. I think the only reason she started being nicer was because she hoped I would help her cater her wedding. For free."

"What? Free?"

"Yes," Sam said. "I couldn't believe it, either. She started by telling me that she wanted me to work for her. When I talked to her about it, she hinted that I should give her the service free of charge because she had already paid for their stay at the guesthouse upfront."

"Wow," I said. "That's awkward."

"Yeah, it was. I didn't give her an answer. I've been avoiding her since," Sam said, as Trouble bumped his furry head against her palm.

"I wonder if that's what she was fighting about with that other woman. The redhead?"

"Redhead?" Sam asked.

"We saw Honey and some woman arguing the other day, but we're not sure who she is. She wasn't from Carmel Springs," I said.

Sam stroked Trouble absentmindedly, her gaze dancing toward the ocean again, then the clouds gathering overhead, the setting sun casting its oranges and pinks along the sky. "Honey's wedding planner was a redhead. What was her name? We were only briefly introduced after Honey and William arrived, and she wasn't at the house much."

Bee sat straighter.

"It explains why she needs a new one, after a fight like that." And the wedding planner had seemed angry as a viper on a hot tin roof. Could she have taken exception to

Honey's vile attitude? She might be a suspect. "So this wedding planner, she wasn't staying in the guesthouse?"

"No," Sam said. "I don't know where she's staying. I haven't seen her in days."

"Interesting," Bee said, drawing the word out.

"I hope I haven't said too much."

"I don't think you have," I replied. "The whole town is probably wild with speculation." And I had to hope that the speculation didn't extend to the food truck. But that was too much to wish for after Jones's treatment this afternoon.

Either way, Honey's murder was a mystery I definitely wanted to solve. What if another guest at Sam's place had done it? Might we be sleeping next door to a murderer?

I settled back and minded the view rather than the conversation going on between Bee and Sam. What was the next step? Figuring out who would've had access to the crime scene. There had been two doors in and out of the kitchen. Who had used them? And was it normal for the town hall to remain unlocked all day?

Seven

DRIVING THE FOOD TRUCK TO THE BEACH AT 8:00
a.m. was a force of habit now, given that I didn't make any
sales most mornings, and Bee was a total grump about
having to wake up early. But there was nothing more reju-
venating than the fresh scent of the sea air, even if the quiet
was broken by the odd squawk of a gull.

"So," Bee said, as she leaned against one of the coun-
ters in the food truck, sipping on a mug of steaming hot
coffee, "what do you want to make this week?"

"For the truck?"

"No, for our impromptu trip to the moon."

"Oof. Somebody didn't get out of bed on the right
side this morning."

Bee sipped her coffee rather than replying, but there
was a twinkle in her eye.

"I'm not sure," I said, after a minute. "I like the idea of the vanilla cupcake with a creamy caramel filling and the caramel frosting on top. They smelled delicious when we made them the other day."

"And I can teach you how to make the filling. It's not difficult. I wanted to check whether you were interested in making something with marzipan."

I pulled a face. "That's a terrible segue into talking about the murder."

"I know. I was too tired to come up with a nice one." She lifted her cup. "Too much coffee. Too much seagull ambient noise."

"They don't bother me that much."

Bee shook her head. "Another anomaly to go with your early morning rising," Bee said. "But really, what do you think about Honey and the wedding planner?"

We'd talked late into the night about it but came to no conclusions. We'd retired with the promise of continuing our chat and investigation the next day.

"I think we need to find out exactly who could get in and out of that town hall. And if they had any cameras. If they did, the murderer might have been caught on tape, and we won't need to worry about solving the case."

"They didn't have any cameras," Bee said, drawing her cellphone from the front pocket of her apron. She set down her coffee and came over. "See?"

I flicked through the pictures on her phone, focusing on the corners of the kitchen rather than Honey's body on the tiles. "You're right. No cameras. That complicates things a bit."

"And look at this," Bee said, gesturing to the back door. "See the lock? It's rusted shut. There's no way the killer came through the back or left through it either."

"Which means they must have gone out of the front." My eyes widened. "What if someone saw them leaving?" Though that didn't help us much. Short of asking all the store owners in the street if they'd seen anything, we didn't have much of a lead. And I doubted many folks in Carmel Springs would be open to questioning from two strangers.

"Maybe we should go back." Bee bent and switched on the oven to warm it up for another morning of baking. "To the town hall."

"Maybe. I don't know. Usually, it stays locked, right?"

"But who would have the keys?"

"The mayor? A maintenance person? Someone who looks after the place, like a caretaker?" I asked.

"Then we need to find out who that is and talk to them. That's our next step." Bee was so sure of herself when it came to investigations and baking, and I couldn't help envying her. "But we'll deal with that later. Let's make ourselves some cupcakes to banish the dead-body blues."

"You have a way with words," I said. "Has anyone ever told you that?"

We set to work, Bee standing at my shoulder and directing me as I made the caramel cream filling. It was therapeutic work, and the end result was delicious—sweet but not sugary, creamy, light and tasting of caramel.

I was tempted to sit down on one of the benches that overlooked the beach and feast on the filling alone. But we made the cupcakes as well, and Bee showed me how to whip up an equally light and delicious frosting. We waited until the cupcakes had cooled, the sweet vanilla scent mingling with the salt on the breeze, then filled the cupcakes and frosted them. I placed the finishing touch on each cupcake with a blob of pure caramel on top.

"Wow," I said. "My mouth's watering."

"It's not like we have any customers to serve," Bee replied. "Let's have one."

One of the rules I'd given myself after leaving New York was that I'd take each opportunity as it presented itself and enjoy every day. That included vanilla-caramel cupcakes. I snagged one out of our display case.

The caramel filling erupted from the cupcake, and I groaned. "These are amazing."

"I'm sold." Millie, the all-smiles editor of the paper, had appeared in front of the food truck's window. "Those smell delish. Mind if I purchase one?"

"You can have as many as you like," I said, placing my cupcake to one side, and then washing my hands. I slipped on the plastic gloves I used to serve customers then extracted one of the cupcakes and placed it in a box. "It's good to see you again, Millie."

"And you, dear. Particularly since you've clearly whipped up something delectable for me to sample," Millie replied, accepting the box and tendering a few dollars. "I see business is still quiet. Has my food critic come over to see you yet?"

"No," I said. "Unfortunately not."

"I'm sure he'll come by soon. Everyone's still a bit freaked out after yesterday," Millie said, popping open the lid of the box then lifting the cupcake out and examining it. "Beautiful." She took a bite and her eyelashes fluttered. "Oh my heavens, these are divine."

"It's all Bee," I said. "She's the baker between the two of us."

Bee whapped me on the arm with a dish cloth. "Not true. Ruby's learning more and more every day."

"Both of you clearly know what you're doing. And that makes me furious at that detective."

"Who? Jones?" I asked.

"Hobbit," Bee murmured.

Millie giggled, but her expression sobered quickly.

43

"He's been very loud about the fact that he found you two at another crime scene."

"It's not like we're actively seeking them out," I replied. "It just seems to happen."

"Dead bodies dropping in our path," Bee agreed, "like we're baking grim reapers."

"Bee, that's not the type of marketing slogan we want out in the world."

Millie laughed again. "You two are hilarious. You've got to come over and have some coffee at my place. Coffee and gossip. Speaking of which, guess what I heard."

"What?" I asked.

Bee poured three mugs of coffee and handed one over to Millie.

"Thank you, dear," she said, accepting it. "That Honey and her dear fiancé had an argument the night before the murder."

"They did?" Bee frowned. "We didn't hear them, and we would have. We'd been hearing them argue all week."

"Now, that's a hot slice of gossip," Millie said, taking a bite of her cupcake and chewing enthusiastically. "But they weren't in the guesthouse when this particular argument took place. They were in the Chowder Hut down on the beach. See, there?"

I peered out of the window in the direction Millie had

pointed. It was opposite the pier, on the street overlooking the waves, elevated on a rocky outcropping.

"Great restaurant, and now, the scene of a potential pre-murder. What do you ladies think?" Millie asked.

"No idea," I said.

Bee kept her peace as well.

But we definitely had our next lead. And a nice place to go to dinner too.

Eight

"ARE YOU SURE YOU WON'T COME WITH US, SAM?"
I buttoned up my overcoat in the front hall of the guesthouse. Trouble rubbed his calico face against my ankles,
purring. *Meow.* I bent and picked him up, heedless of the
fur he'd leave behind on my black coat.

"I'm not sure if everyone's going out for dinner or
not," Sam said from behind her antique reception desk.
She swiveled to and fro in her chair. "I can't leave in case
one of the others comes back. Poor William has been
locked upstairs all evening."

"I heard him crying earlier," Bee whispered.

"I think he loved her very much. Of course he did.
They were engaged." Sam removed a Kleenex from a pack
on the desk and blew her nose. "Oh, it's so tragic. One of
my guests murdered. I can't believe it."

"It will be all right," I said with confidence I didn't have. "Listen, we'll bring you something from the restaurant. What would you like?"

"You don't have to do that."

"It would be our pleasure," Bee said. "What will it be?"

"I'd love a lobster roll if it's not too much trouble. I can give you money for it."

"No, no," I said. "It's on us." I gave Trouble a quick kiss on the head, promising that I'd bring him something as well, then set him down. He promptly sprawled across the keyboard of Sam's laptop, stretching out his kitty paws.

"You be careful out there."

Sam's words followed us out into the icy evening. We trooped toward the food truck, our breath misting in front of our faces. It was simply too chilly to walk, though I would have loved the exercise.

"I wonder if the servers at the Chowder Hut will be as forthcoming as the ones at the Lobster Shack were," I said, as I steered us into one of the last parking spaces in front of the restaurant.

We clambered out of the truck and entered the Chowder Hut. My hopes were high. We hadn't gone to any restaurants lately, and I was definitely in the mood for seafood. How could one not be after spending the day at the beach?

A server appeared, two menu cards pinned to his side. "Good evening, ladies. Table for two?"

"Yeah," Bee said. "We'd like to sit there." She pointed to a booth at the back of the restaurant. The interior was decked out in sea-greens and ashen white furniture, with a lobster trap sitting in one corner and buoys hanging from the walls.

We followed the server to our table with high-backed leather booth chairs that would give us some privacy.

The savory scents of grilled fish, the tang of lemon, and the richness of garlic-butter sauce drifted through the restaurant. My stomach protested, and I opened my menu and scanned the food on offer.

"Yummy." I trailed my finger down the page. I paused. Bee hadn't opened her menu. She hadn't even glanced at it and that was unlike her. She was even more of a foodie than I was. "What's up?"

"Look there," she whispered, nodding toward the raised center area of the restaurant.

Two people, a brunette wearing crimson lipstick and a man who had to be in his early thirties sat there, leaning back in their chairs, as far away from each other as possible. My eyes widened. It was Jessie, the maid of honor from the wedding, and Richard, William's brother. Or was it William?

Gosh, the fact that they were twins complicated

things. But no, he had a mole on his right cheek, above his mouth. It was the brother.

Why were they at dinner together when they so clearly didn't want to be?

"What do you think they're doing?" I whispered.

"I don't know, but there's a reason I chose this table. Ten bucks says we overhear what they're talking about."

We fell silent, and I scooched closer to the edge of my seat, listening hard. Now, as a journalist, I'd never used underhanded tactics like this. I'd had integrity. But I was officially free of those chains. I could do whatever it took to gather information. Even if it was a bit unorthodox to listen in on someone's conversation.

"—don't understand why you think that."

"It's not about what I think," Richard said quietly. "It's about what I know."

"Is that a threat?"

Richard rolled his eyes.

I lifted my menu and pretended to scan it, but I kept them in my peripheral vision. Bee took a sip of her water, staring directly ahead instead of at the pair.

"Of course it's not a threat. What do you think I am, stupid?"

"I wasn't going to say anything, but if you're admitting it..."

"Very funny, Jessie. You've always had a big mouth,"

Richard said. "And that's exactly the reason I know what I know."

"Can you keep your voice down?" she hissed. "Someone might hear you."

"Do I look like I care?" Richard lifted his soda from the table and drank deeply. He let out a loud burp.

Rude.

The handsome twin laughed under his breath. "So, what do you think I should do with this information?"

Jessie's lips twitched. "Just shut up."

"I don't think I will," he said. "I think everyone should know that your friend, your evil, mean friend, didn't want to marry my brother at all. She was only in it for his money. Everyone's feeling so sorry for Honey, meanwhile it was my brother who was trapped in a relationship with her."

"You don't know what you're talking about," Jessie hissed.

"I heard her tell you. I heard it loud and clear, and I'm going to let everyone in this town know that she's trash."

"Stop it. Stop talking about her like that." Tears streamed down Jessie's tan cheeks. "You don't understand what we were talking about. You don't—" She scraped her chair back and rose from the table.

"Don't leave yet," Richard said. "I'm only getting started."

But Jessie had had enough. She ran from the restaurant, bashing our server out of her path. A stunned silence followed her departure, broken by the gentle parlor music.

"Sorry about that, folks," Richard called out, raising both hands. "The missus can't handle a little confrontation."

None of the other diners returned his smile. Slowly, everyone got back to their meals or talk, but gazes kept darting over to Richard. It made it much easier for me to spy on him. He seemed positively merry, now, as if he'd gotten exactly what he wanted.

"Can you believe that? How rude."

"I can believe that we need to talk to Jessie about this," Bee said. "There's always two sides to a story."

And to a murder.

Nine

"THAT WAS A LOVELY NIGHT." I DIRECTED THE truck down the road toward the Oceanside. We weren't too far from our temporary home. The guesthouse had started feeling like a place I could live in. Of course, it would be short-lived. If we didn't start earning money on the food truck, we wouldn't be able to afford it for much longer.

"Lovely is one way of wording it. The food was scrumptious, but the atmosphere..."

"What do you make of it?" We'd talked over the argument between Jessie and Richard already, but I couldn't quit thinking about it. Not even the chowder appetizer had scraped it from my mind, nor the delicious fresh-caught fish and fries.

"That Jessie clearly has something to hide," Bee said,

grasping the three boxes on her lap so they wouldn't wobble and spill their contents over the seat. One contained Sam's lobster roll, and the other two carried our desserts—chocolate raspberry mousse cakes.

I pulled into our parking spot outside the guesthouse, the headlights of the truck flaring along the side of the house and illuminating the windows briefly. They were dark, the curtains drawn. Everyone had gone to bed early, doubtlessly because of what had happened to Honey.

"We should offer our condolences to Jessie and William," I said. "And Richard too. Though, it doesn't seem like he's affected by Honey's death."

"People deal with grief in strange ways," Bee said. "I once knew a man who lost his wife in a boating accident and went on a two-month fishing trip to celebrate her passing."

"That's... I don't know what that is."

"Inappropriate comes to mind," Bee replied. "I don't think they had the best marriage."

"What happened after he came back from his trip?"

"He brought back a new wife and child. Shameful, really. He was seventy years old."

"Good heavens." I tried not to judge, but that kind of behavior made it difficult.

"Oh, don't worry, he got his just deserts. She left him for a younger model the next year. And then he passed away. And then she went on a fishing trip in her new beau's yacht. Which goes to prove the saying, 'all's well that ends well.' Wait, no, that's not the saying."

"Every dog gets his day?" I suggested.

"That's the one."

I cut the lights of the food truck, and the engine ticked as it cooled. "Come on," I said, "let's forget about fishing trips and have some mousse cake instead. We can talk about the mystery."

"Mousse cake and murder. You know, that sounds like a good title for a book."

I chuckled and removed the keys from the ignition. A flicker of movement caught my eye, and I looked up. What had that been? The outside of the guesthouse was different, but I couldn't place how.

"What is it?" Bee asked. "What are you looking at?"

"I don't know. I thought I saw something move—" I gasped. "There, look!"

A figure stood next to the side of the guesthouse. They were tall and appeared to be leaning against one of the windows, hands cupped around their face.

"That's not one of the guests," Bee said. "They're wearing a mask."

The murderer? Panic closed its cold hand around my heart. "W-what? What do we...?"

"Wait here, Ruby. I'll handle this." Bee clunked open

her door and shot out, her high-heeled boots inhibiting her in no way. "Hey! You! Stop right there."

"Bee, don't."

But it was too late. The Peeping Tom—or Tina—had heard her. They darted back from the window and into the bushes.

I switched on the truck's headlights and caught the tail end of a sneaker disappearing from view. Bee chased after them, diving into the scraggly bushes that flanked the guesthouse.

"Not again," I muttered.

Bee had a terrible habit of rushing after intruders. And I had an equally bad one of panicking at inopportune moments. My mother had always teased me about it, and we'd dubbed it "Beaning." Because we'd get so caught up in the moment, we'd start acting like Mr. Bean, rushing this way and that and catching ourselves mid-stride.

"Not today." I slipped out of the truck. "Bee!"

I hurried down the side of the building, my jacket hardly sufficient at guarding against the fall chill, and stopped at the point where Bee and the intruder had disappeared. The bushes were parted, the branches on one were broken where they'd crashed through.

"Bee?" My palms were slick.

The beams from the truck's headlights lengthened my shadow in the sand around the side of the guesthouse, and

I took a breath, trying to calm myself. What if the peeper leaped from the shadows and attacked? What if they had more of my marzipan on hand?

The thought was so ridiculous it brought a smile to my lips, and that helped keep the Beaning at bay. "Bee!" I yelled.

"I'm here." Her cry was close by. She emerged from the bushes at a point farther down the trail, picking leaves off her coat. "Couldn't catch up to them. I'm not as fit as I used to be."

"You shouldn't have been chasing after them in the first place."

"And you're contaminating a potential crime scene."

"Huh?"

"You're standing a foot away from where they were. Look."

I spotted a pair of sneaker prints in the dirt underneath the living room window. "Oh."

"Oh indeed," Bee said. "I wish I'd gotten a good look at them, but the mask hid everything."

"What type of mask was it?"

"Halloween mask. A vampire or something. And they had a hoodie on too," Bee said, fisting her palm. "Gosh, if only I'd—"

I lifted a hand. "Look there." The truck's lights had

caught a glint of something beneath the window, right in front of the shoeprints in the sand.

Bee crouched down and peered at it. "Well, I'll be."

"What is it?"

She shifted, the crinkling of her coat loud in the hush. "A ring." Bee pulled her gloves from her pocket and slipped them on. She reached for the ring.

"Shouldn't we call the police?"

Bee blew a raspberry. "And tell them what? That somebody dropped their ring outside the window? You know what Detective Jones will say about that. Or rather, how he'll laugh in our faces for mentioning it."

She had a point. "We should at least report that someone was creeping around the guesthouse."

"Sure, we can do that, but I doubt it will serve the investigation. Jones will dismiss it like he dismissed us the last time." Bee held up the ring. "Oh wow. It's an engagement ring."

Our gazes met. "Are you thinking what I'm thinking?"

"Only if you're thinking that we need to eat our mousse cakes and have a serious discussion about this."

I blinked. "No, that the ring might belong to Honey."

"Hmm. Maybe." But Bee didn't seem too sure. "Why would the creeper have had it?"

"What if the murderer removed the ring from her hand?"

Bee raised an eyebrow. "That's interesting. And we can check that fact. I have those pictures of the crime scene on my phone."

"Let's talk about it upstairs." The mousse cakes were calling my name as well, and standing outside talking about the murder was hardly inconspicuous.

"I hope it's not her ring, because if it is, we do need to report this to Jones." Bee sighed. "And you know how much I'll be looking forward to that."

Ten

AND THERE IT WAS. OR RATHER, THERE IT wasn't.

The picture on Bee's phone gave me all types of chills, but I forced myself to focus on Honey's left hand and the empty ring finger. "It has to be her engagement ring then," I whispered.

The gravity of the statement struck me, and I plopped down in one of the floral armchairs and grabbed my boxed up mousse cake. I tucked in, using the plastic fork the server had kindly packed with it and relished the tang of raspberry and the richness of the chocolate.

It helped calm my nerves. "It has to have been the murderer outside that window," I said, between chews. "But why were they holding the ring? And if it was so important, why would they just leave it there after they dropped it?"

"Hmm." Bee pursed her lips and wriggled them from side-to-side. "We don't know for sure that that's true, Ruby. This ring might've been lying in the sand outside that window for a while. Honey might have thrown it out during one of her fights with William."

"One thing I learned during my tenure as a journalist was that the most simple and rational solution was usually the correct one."

"Why would the killer have removed the ring then come back with it in hand?"

"I don't know," I said. "I really don't. But we have to call Jones."

"Not until after I've had my cake," Bee replied. "I'll need all the sugar I can get if I'm going to deal with him again." She ate a bite of chocolatey goodness, setting her phone aside. "Ah, that's better."

"Delicious, isn't it? We should do something like this on the truck."

"Not that it will help if there are no customers buying."

"Now, Bee, you can't let Jones get to you like this. He's put you in a bad mood, and we haven't even called him yet."

"Yes, well—" she cut off, frowning, and tilted her head

to the side.

"What is it?"

Bee set her box down on the coffee table and rose. "Crying," she whispered. "I hear crying. Don't you?"

I listened hard.

The gentle sob and hiccup seemed to be coming from … the wall! I'd had more than enough fear for one night. If the guesthouse was haunted with the ghost of a weeping woman, I'd check out and move on so fast the detective's head would spin.

Bee, once again, didn't seem afraid. She approached the wall and pressed her ear to it, tucking her silver hair out of the way. "It's coming from the room next to yours."

"Who's next door?"

"There's only one way to find out," Bee said and pushed off from the wall. "I have a hunch, though."

"Jessie?" It would make sense that she'd be upset after what had happened to Honey and at the restaurant with Richard.

I followed Bee out into the hall, and we knocked on the weeping woman's door.

It opened, and it was, indeed, Jessie who appeared, her brown locks tucked back behind her ears, and her makeup streaked. Long trails of mascara ran down her tan cheeks, and her lipstick had smudged at the corners of her mouth.

"Hello," Bee said.

"We heard you crying. Are you all right?"

"I'm fine," she croaked.

"We wanted to offer our condolences for your loss." I placed a hand on her shoulder.

Jessie broke down into a flurry of sobs and threw herself into my arms. I hugged her and patted her back, mouthing the word "coffee" at Bee over the woman's shoulder.

"Right," Bee said. "Let's get you something warm and fortifying." She entered Jessie's room, and I followed, guiding the distraught maid of honor along and sitting her down in an armchair.

Her room was slightly bigger than mine, with a queen-sized bed and a balcony she could exit onto to look out on the ocean. Still, I wouldn't have traded places with her in a million years. How sad it had to be to lose a best friend the way she had.

"It was just so sudden," Jessie said, dabbing under her eyes with a Kleenex that was so frayed and used, bits of white tissue crumbled from its ends into her lap.

I lifted the fresh pack off her coffee table and handed it to her, taking a seat myself. "It really is terrible," I said. "I can't imagine how you must be feeling."

"She was such a ray of sunshine in my life." Jessie sniveled and dabbed, sniveled and dabbed. "Whenever I needed help, Honey was there. She wasn't the easiest person to get along with for other folks, but she was so nice to me. She was my friend. And now she's gone. What am I supposed to do without her?"

Bee opened her mouth then closed it again. Likely, she'd had a sarcastic response on the tip of her tongue, but even she could tell that now wasn't the time for it.

I patted Jessie on the arm. "We haven't spent much time with the other guests, but even we could see that you two were close."

"We were." Jessie blew her nose. "I don't think what happened actually hit me until tonight. Until Richard—" Her face grew red all over.

"Until he embarrassed you in the Chowder Hut," Bee finished for her. "Sorry to say it, dear, but we were there. He was being super rude."

"Yes, he was," Jessie said. "Mean creature. He did that on purpose, just to embarrass me. Actually, no, that's not why."

"Why then?" I asked.

"Because he's trying to hide the truth from everyone. That he's probably the one who killed her."

Bee dropped a teaspoon with a clatter.

"Why do you think that?" I asked, finding my voice again. "I mean, that's quite a thing to say about someone."

"Yes, I know it is. But I'm sure he had something to do with it." Jessie scooched to the edge of the armchair, her bloodshot eyes shifting. "Honey told me that William had forced her to include Richard in her will." Jessie paused for effect. "Obviously, William's well off, but he's been having some trouble with his businesses lately. And Honey? She's an Instagram model. She makes loads of money. I warned her about William, but she wouldn't listen, and now... well."

"This isn't your fault," I said.

But the fact that Honey had changed her will to include Richard was a big deal. What if Richard had wanted Honey dead because he was in dire financial straits?

"You think that Richard would have been desperate enough for money to murder Honey?" Bee asked.

"Of course. Richard is a scumbag. I don't think he's worked a day in his entire life. If there was an easy way for him to ride their coattails he would've, but I know for a fact that Honey told William, after the wedding, she didn't want to see Richard around anymore. She didn't want him in her life."

And if that was the case, what better motivation could Richard have had?

Eleven

"ARE YOU READY FOR THIS, RUBES?" BEE ASKED AS she packed vanilla-caramel cupcakes into a box. "I know this might be too much for you."

"Hey, I used to be a journalist. I can handle this." But it was one thing to research a story, to question people or interview them, but to follow them? Well, I'd done that too, but never with a suspect in a murder case.

"You'll be fine." Bee gave her a gap-toothed smile.

I paused, studying my friend. She was so on top of everything when it came to cupcakes and murders. "You seem comfortable with the concept of tailing a suspect, Bee."

My friend shrugged. "One does what they have to do," she said, mysteriously.

I had never pried into her history, but the curiosity

bug had bitten me. Still, I respected her privacy and wouldn't ask. When she was ready to tell me, she would.

"I hope it's not a waste of time," I said. "What if today's the day that Millie's food critic comes to check out the truck?" We had opened the side window and parked in front of the guesthouse instead of at the beach today. And for good reason—we needed to keep our eye on the comings and goings of one particular guesthouse resident.

Richard Hall.

Our prime suspect after the discovery of the changes to Honey's will. Assuming the changes had gone through. What if Jessie had been lying about that to remove suspicion from her?

"I don't think we're going to have any customers soon," Bee said. "It's unfortunate, but at least we can use the time to figure out what happened to Honey. Here, have a cupcake. It will cheer you up."

I took one of the vanilla-caramels gratefully and peeled back the paper. The first bite was heaven, and the sweetness did help me chill out. It wasn't as if we had any proof that Richard had done it. Yet. And our run-in with Detective Jones early this morning had only added to my determination.

He had taken the engagement ring, reluctantly noted down our encounter, and then left us with the warning to stay out of his investigation.

Perfectly pleasant as usual.

"These are so good." I finished off my cupcake and disposed of my paper.

"If you do say so yourself. You helped, you know. You can take credit for your hard work."

"I hardly did anything. You're the one who came up with the recipe. Honestly, Bee, I don't know what I'd do without you. Probably not own a bakery on wheels."

"You'd have less trouble with Jones, that's for sure. He's definitely taken a disliking to me. I suppose that's my own fault, but I can't regret it." Bee closed up the box of cupcakes. "Are you ready to go?"

We planned on taking the cupcakes to William and squeezing him for information. Without being too obvious about it, of course. I had a natural gift for two things: panicking and getting information out of people in a friendly and easy manner.

We'd overheard that Richard and William would be meeting right now—their hush-hush conversation over breakfast had traveled no matter how they whispered. And that meant we could question them both, and when Richard got spooked, tail him.

"Let's do it," I said.

The words had barely left my mouth when the front door of the guesthouse clapped open. Richard marched onto the porch, drawing a cigarette and lighter from his pocket. He paused and lit up then puffed out a cloud of smoke.

Bee and I stood deathly still, her clutching the box, and me trying not to stare too openly.

Richard didn't spot us but walked off down the street at a leisurely pace.

"Where do you think he's going?" Bee asked.

"Should we?"

"I think so." Bee left the cupcakes on the counter, and I rushed around and closed up the truck. Quick as we could, we were off down the road after him.

Richard had already reached the corner. He took a left without looking back.

And so the chase began. If it could be counted as a chase when the man being pursued strolled along like he had nowhere in particular to be.

Bee and I kept back, talking softly in case he looked over his shoulder or decided to turn around. But he didn't, and he took a squiggly path through Carmel Springs and into streets with brick houses with crumbling garden walls and stained curtains in their windows.

"Should we turn back?" I asked.

"When we're so close to finding out where he's going? I don't think so."

A half an hour of walking had passed, and the sun had reached its zenith by the time Richard dipped into the parking lot of the Go-To Drinking Spot, a bar with a worn sign attached to its brick face. The windows were grayed out with dirt or a tint, but the low thump of music spilled out of it when he entered.

I stopped on the street. Bee did too.

"Well," I said, "I don't see myself going in there any time soon."

"One has to make sacrifices in pursuit of the truth, dear."

"I would do anything for the truth, but I won't do that."

Bee chuckled but started off across the parking lot, and I followed. Bars had never been my thing, especially not ones that looked like this. The cars parked outside were mostly in states of rust or disrepair, and there were stains on the parking lot that I didn't want identified.

Bee pushed open the door and entered.

The music thumped loudly from speakers in the corners of the room. A bar with a dusty mirror behind it held glasses and bottles of alcohol. Men and women sat on stools talking idly, most of them in ragged clothes.

"OK," Bee said, "so maybe coming in here wasn't the best idea, after all."

One of the burliest guys in the places had spotted us and started stroking his long, gray beard. And Richard? He was nowhere to be seen.

"Where did he go?" I asked.

"No idea, but I won't be storming through here asking questions." Bee touched a hand to her purse and fiddled with the golden latch set in brown leather. "Let's go."

We exited the bar fast and set off across the street.

A door banged behind us. "Hey!" It was the gray-bearded man. "Hey, you. I know who you are."

"Who?" I asked.

"Keep walking," Bee said, urgently. "Don't look back."

"Come back here." The man's gruff calls followed us onto the sidewalk. "What's the matter, Beatrice, you don't want to talk to me?"

The fact that he'd used Bee's full name came as such a shock, I stopped mid-stride. "He knows you, Bee."

"Keep walking, I said." Bee's neck and décolletage had pinked. "Just ignore him."

"Beatrice."

But Bee wouldn't stop walking, and I chased along beside her, glancing back over my shoulder at the gray-bearded man. After a while, he stopped following and stood with his hands on his hips, shaking his head.

"Bee," I said.

"It's nothing, Ruby. Just an old friend."

"Here? You didn't tell me you'd been to Maine before."

"I haven't," she replied, stiffly. "It's just a coincidence. Let's forget about it and focus on the case, all right?"

And that was the end of that. All we'd garnered from our expedition was the knowledge that Richard hung out in a seedy bar just outside of Carmel Springs, and that Bee had friends in strange places. Ones she didn't want to talk to or about.

Twelve

Bee had retired to her bedroom after the strange incident at the bar. I left her to it rather than bothering her about what had happened. Doubtless she wouldn't appreciate the interference.

It also gave me time to wash the truck and to steal another of the cupcakes. Under normal circumstances, I would never have snacked on our product, but since no one was buying, I enjoyed the guilty pleasure rather than mentally reprimanding myself for it.

Clouds blotted out the sun intermittently, and I finished up my food truck once-over after a quick rinse from Samantha's garden hose.

The back of the guesthouse, with its comfy porch and chairs, called my name, and I rounded the side of the house, stopping to peer at the spot where the shoeprints sat beneath the living room window.

Why? Why had someone been peering inside? Who had they been looking for? And if it was the murderer, why would they have come back to the guesthouse when they'd already done the deed?

Yuck, I hated thinking about a murder in those terms.

I stomped onto the back porch and settled my tired bones into a chair, resting my hands in my lap. Trouble padded out of the open sliding door and hopped into my lap, purring for attention. I stroked his ears.

"I can always count on you to lighten the mood," I said.

Samantha came out of the back door as well, the local newspaper clasped in her hand, her gaze scanning the front page. She took two absent-minded steps toward the swinging seat then stopped, shaking her head. "I don't believe it," she whispered. "This is terrible."

"What is?"

Samantha shrieked and threw the paper at me. Thankfully, it fluttered to the ground before it got very far. Trouble hissed and hopped around in my lap, his little claws coming out and his back arching, tail bottle-brush thick.

"Sorry," I said. "I take it you didn't see me sitting here?"

"Oh, Ruby, it's you. Thank goodness. For one horrible moment, I was sure it was... you know."

"Someone else?"

"Right." She picked up the paper and folded it messily, then sat down on the swinging seat. "I'm on edge, as you can probably tell. And I can't believe what I just read in the paper. They've labeled my guesthouse as a 'murder hotel.' I've never been so upset in my life."

"Really?"

"See for yourself."

I picked up the paper and opened it, scanning the article.

Trouble at Maine's Murder Hotel...

"Oh wow, that's a headline if ever I saw one." Whoever had written this had gone in on the guesthouse. The article was well-sourced with information about Honey Wilson and her fiancé.

"How am I going to draw in new customers at this rate? People will avoid the guesthouse."

"Or you'll draw in a crowd of people who are intrigued by murders. You know, you get that crowd of folks who hop from place to place seeking out the history behind local murders. Kind of like an unhealthy obsession."

Samantha groaned and covered her face. "All I wanted was to fix up my grandmother's guesthouse and share how amazing this place is with everyone."

"Don't worry, Sam," I said, flicking the paper's front page with two fingers. "This is just an angle."

"What do you mean?"

"Listen to this," I said, clearing my throat and finding the relevant paragraph. "According to police reports, Ms. Wilson, an Instagram model and self-proclaimed beauty, was found in the kitchen of the town hall. It appeared there had been a struggle between her and the killer, whose identity remains unknown. Suspicions arise, however, regarding the other guests at the hotel in town."

Sam groaned again.

"Two of the occupants are not originally from Carmel Springs and were associated with a previous murder investigation in the town. Miss Ruby Holmes and Miss Beatrice Pine run a local food truck and had recently been hired to cater the victim's wedding. By a stroke of sheer madness, it appears that the murder weapon itself was the marzipan made by the baking duo. Speculation is rife as to whether these ladies are involved." I grew hot under the collar at the insinuation.

"Oh no. They can't really think you did that, can they, Ruby?"

"It doesn't matter what anyone thinks other than Detective Jones." Not a good portent for either Bee or me. "My point is, Sam, the whole 'murder hotel' thing is just an angle. The writer hasn't penned anything here that pins the murder on you or even relates it that much to the guesthouse. They called it a hotel, for heaven's sake."

"What does that mean?"

"That the paper will move on to bigger and better things when more evidence arises," I said. "I wouldn't worry about it too much if I were you."

"You think so?" Sam asked, drawing her yellow-blonde hair from her face as the breeze whipped it around.

"I know so." But the fact that the reports were so vicious and damning told me that solving this case had to take top priority. There had been a struggle in the kitchen, according to the paper. Did that mean that the attacker might have pulled the engagement ring off?

Perhaps it had been an accident. Or perhaps the crime had been motivated out of a lust for money. That pointed back to Richard again. Richard was tall. But so was Jessie. And William. But what if it had been none of them and instead had been an outside attacker? What about the redhead we'd seen arguing with Honey only a day or two before the murder?

"Are you all right, Ruby?"

"Yes, yes, I'm fine."

"I'm sorry the reporter wrote that about you and Bee. Nothing could be further from the truth," Sam said. "I'm a good judge of character, and I know you two wouldn't do anything to hurt anyone. Ever."

"Thanks." I didn't need the comfort, but she was such a sweetheart. And Trouble purring and settling in my lap brought a sense of warmth too.

What about Bee?

Therein lay another mystery. Gosh, I had been so sure I'd be rid of the hunt for truth when I'd bought my food truck and started revamping it. And now, I was on the road with my friend, and mystery had followed us all the way to another state.

"I'm going to fix myself a cup of coffee and some cookies. Would you like some?" Sam asked.

"That would be great, thank you."

She left me with Trouble. At least Sam seemed happier than she had when she'd come out onto the back deck.

The afternoon had worn on, and the sky had grown dull with gray clouds, thick with coming rain. A lone figure appeared on the sandy path leading through the bushes. Richard strode toward the back of the guesthouse, hands in the pockets of his jeans. He grinned at me and nodded then ducked inside, trailing the odor of cigarette smoke.

Was it a coincidence that he had taken a different path back to the Oceanside? And what had that grin meant? Did he know we'd followed him?

Samantha returned with the cookies and coffee, and I dismissed the thoughts for now.

Thirteen

"IF THAT'S NOT A HIT PIECE OF AN ARTICLE, I'VE never seen one," Bee said, her legs crossed and one of her fluffy bunny-ear slippers dangling from the tips of her toes. "Seriously. How were we involved in the last murder? That makes it sounds like we should be charged for it, not like we helped solve it."

It was after dinner, and I had tactfully avoided talking about our run-in with the bearded guy earlier. There were more important things to discuss. Like Richard's walking routes, the article, and the victim herself.

"But it's interesting, don't you think?" I lifted my mug of coffee and took a sip. "What they said about the struggle. If only we knew who she struggled with. From what we've heard, she wasn't well-liked."

"Hmm, true." Bee folded the paper and tossed it aside, lifting her mug to her lips after. "Here's our problem," she said, "we don't know enough about the victim to warrant a true suspect list. We know that Richard and Jessie were fighting. Richard had motivation. William has been absolutely silent for days, and Jessie is visibly distraught. Those are our only suspects."

"And the wedding planner."

"Right. But if Honey was so hated, there might be suspects we're missing."

I thought it over. Trouble poked his head around the bathroom door and meowed at me. He had a knack for squeezing through nooks and crannies, as most cats did. Even when I was sure I'd closed every window, he found a way into my room, and thus Bee's too, since they were connected by a shared bathroom.

"Here, Trouble," I said.

"Oh, well, now you're just asking for it." Bee laughed.

Trouble hopped onto the arm of the chair, and I stroked him, eliciting a few purrs and a scratch.

"Let's research Honey," I said. "I've heard twice now that she's an Instagram model. She can't be too hard to find online. Maybe we'll find articles about her or more information that could lead us to a suspect."

"Good idea."

I brought out my phone and shifted to the chair next to Bee's so she'd be able to see my screen. It took about two seconds of searching to find Honey's account and the countless photos that skirted the line of inappropriate.

"Good heavens," Bee said, shading her eyes. "I'm not a prude, but that's just ... is that a flesh-colored bikini?"

"Let's hope so," I replied, skipping through the images. I frowned, slowing as I scrolled upward again. One of the most recent pictures, right at the top of her profile, was different from the others. "What's this?"

"Do I want to know? Is it a flesh-colored dress?"

"No," I said, "and I believe the correct term is 'nude.'"

"That's serendipitous. Or ironic. I can't decide which."

"It's one of those open-letter posts," I said, clicking on the image. It was basically a block of text that Honey had written up on her notepad. She'd snapped a screenshot of it and uploaded it for her followers to view. "Don't worry, you can look."

Bee peeked out from behind her fingers. "Ah, that's better. The purity of the written word."

"Don't be too hasty. We don't know what she's written about."

Bee pinched my arm. "Don't tease me."

We hunched over to read the words on the picture.

I have, like, never been so angry in my whole entire life. You guys don't even understand. So, I hired the best, like, literally the best—

"This is painful to read," Bee said, leaning back in her chair. "Give me the CliffsNotes."

I scanned the text. "Wow."

"What?"

"It's about the wedding planner."

"Oh really?" Bee sat forward again. Trouble meowed at us from the other chair, where he'd seated himself like a king in a throne room filled with his subjects.

"Yes. Apparently, the wedding planner is an expensive and popular professional from Los Angeles. Her name is Gina Josephs. Honey tagged her in the picture and everything."

"I have no idea what that means."

"Basically, that she linked the image with Gina's profile."

"OK. So what did she say about her?" Bee asked.

"It's a flaming takedown of this Gina woman. Apparently, Honey expected more than what she got from the wedding planner. And she's saying that Gina stole money from her by charging a fee at the beginning of the job and that now that Honey's fired her, Gina doesn't want to give the deposit back or something. I don't know, it's quite garbled." I paused. "But she ends the post by saying none of her two million followers should ever use Gina's service."

"So," Bee said, "you're telling me that two million people follow this woman who poses in 'nude' bikinis and dresses?"

"That's the part you find shocking?"

"The whole thing is beyond the pale," she replied. "But it definitely gives us another suspect for our list. What if this Gina woman, who has to be the redhead we saw fighting with Honey... what if she decided to kill Honey for her money?"

"Honey for her money," I said. "That rhymes."

"Not with murder, though. Is it enough motivation?"

"No idea. I'm not an expert by any stretch of the imagination. Do you think we should tell Jones about this? You know, fill him in on what we've found?"

"And endure his deadpan stare and body odor?" Bee asked. "I think not."

"He didn't smell that bad the last time we spoke to him."

"Like a diaper barge under a noon sun off the coast of Florida," Bee replied.

"There's an image." But the clue was there. This wedding planner had been arguing with Honey only the day before the murder. And she wasn't staying in the guesthouse, as far as I knew. We certainly hadn't seen her at lunches or dinners. But then, William hadn't been around lately either. Understandable since he was in mourning.

"We'll have to find out more about this woman," Bee said. "Where she's staying and so on."

"If she's still here. Why would she hang around after being fired by Honey?" I asked.

"Interesting point." Bee stifled a yawn, setting her coffee to one side. "This coffee has tired me out." She was convinced that coffee didn't keep her awake but made her sleepy. It had to be some kind of placebo effect, because I was far too buzzed to be tired.

"Right," I said. "I'll see you in the morning. Sleep tight."

"Don't let the murderers bite." Bee guffawed. "Sorry. I've always had a strange sense of humor."

I waved goodbye and exited the room, Trouble chasing after me. Sam didn't seem to mind when Trouble spent time with the guests. She said he was just as good a judge of character as she was, and he only liked people he trusted.

It was a nice thought that accompanied me into my room. The windows were locked tight, the curtains drawn, and my bed warm from the heated blanket I'd switched on before I'd popped into Bee's room. I shut it off now and sat on the edge of my bed, contemplating my phone.

I wasn't tired in the slightest. The thought of what might have happened to mean Honey dribbled through my mind. *Don't worry, Honey, we'll find out who did this to you.* And then maybe the folks in this town would start paying attention to the food truck at last.

Fourteen

I'D HARDLY GOTTEN A WINK OF SLEEP AFTER THE coffee the night before, but I was up early regardless. The crack of dawn is what Bee would've called it, all while grumbling and flopping around in her slippers until, eventually, I told her she could come down later.

I didn't even bother waking her anymore. Bee was too good of a baker for me to be worried much by what hour she woke, particularly since she was usually up before seven ready to get the baking started.

As long as we were ready by the time we needed to serve customers, why worry? Except, nowadays, there weren't customers to serve. But today would be different. I'd open the truck, and, hopefully, Millie's food critic would come by to try our cakes.

I contemplated that fact, and the discovery of the

wedding planner's dismissal on Honey's profile, while I made myself a morning cup of coffee. Or rather, a 5:00 a.m. cup of coffee. I had had trouble sleeping ever since Daniel, my ex-fiancé, had left. If that was the correct term for it.

It wasn't even like he was on my mind. I just couldn't relax enough to fall asleep. There were so many unanswered questions. Why hadn't he just told me instead of—?

"Stop it," I muttered, pouring a little too much sugar into my coffee. "There's no reason to be thinking about that now."

I sipped my coffee, choosing to stand by my window and look down on the dusk embracing the ocean below. A lone figure jogged along the sands, the moonlight casting the sliver of their shadow on the beach.

The beginnings of dawn appeared—a slight lightening along the horizon. Wouldn't it be nice to live here permanently? I could imagine it ... owning a little restaurant in town and liaising with the locals every day.

While it sounded great, it also gave me the itches. Staying in one place meant connecting with people and making friendships, perhaps even meeting a man. Settling down was not an option for me anymore.

I finished off my coffee and placed my mug next to the

coffee station then grabbed my handbag and let myself out of the room.

The hall was quiet apart from the gentle shuffle of my footsteps on the old house's floor. I ran my hand along the polished railing and took the stairs down to the bottom floor and into the hall. A step that definitely wasn't my own sounded behind me.

Huh?

No one else was usually awake at this time of the morning.

The noise came again, and I searched for it in the darkened hall.

A figure stood near one of the doors to the bottom floor rooms. My throat closed, but I forced myself to remain calm. Just because someone was in the hall didn't mean they were a murderer. They were right across from Richard's room.

Just breathe and think, Ruby. Don't panic this time.

I fished my phone out of my handbag and switched on the screen and flashlight app, directing it toward the person at the door. The blue light illuminated a woman who definitely didn't belong in the guesthouse. A redhead.

I recognized her from the beach the day before Honey's murder.

She straightened, stumbling back at the sight of my phone.

"Hey," I said. "What are you doing here?"

The redhead folded her arms. "I'm not the one snooping around in the middle of the night," she replied.

"I stay here. Do you?"

She hesitated.

"Then I'm not the one snooping, am I? I'm calling the police."

"Good heavens," she said. "There's no need for that. I let myself in with a key." She lifted it out of her pocket. "Jessie gave it to me."

"Jessie?"

"Yeah, Jessie. She's staying here. She was the maid of honor for a wedding I was organizing. My name is Gina."

The way she said it made it sound like she hadn't been fired. But that couldn't possibly be true. It was clear that Honey had made her decision. She'd even cried to us about it.

"You're here to speak to Jessie at five in the morning?" I wasn't convinced. "I'm still calling the cops."

"Go ahead. It doesn't bother me," Gina replied, drawling the words. She touched a finger to her right ear. "I'll tell them the same thing I'm about to tell you. That it's none of your business why I'm here."

I reached over and clicked the hall light on, casting her pale features into sharp relief. She squinted briefly. "It's definitely my business," I said, "since Honey was murdered, and there might still be a killer roaming around in town."

"You're afraid of a murderer?" Gina asked. "That's so cute."

"What's that supposed to mean?" I hadn't particularly liked Honey, but I had to agree with her assessment of Gina here. She was abrasive at best.

"It means that no one wants to murder you," she said. "Nobody even knows who you are. But plenty of people knew Honey and disliked her."

"We're getting off-topic." I could do this. I just had to stick to my guns. Or my cakes. Whatever. "You still haven't told me why you're here."

"Duh, I'm meeting Jessie." Gina gestured to her clothing. She was outfitted in a pair of spandex shorts, a loose T-shirt, and a pair of sneakers. She reached up and tugged on her ear. "We're supposed to be going for a run on the beach. We do this every morning. Not that it's any of your business. Like... what a total intrusion on my privacy."

"Sorry, but everyone's jumpy around here."

"Whatever. I'm going to wait outside. I don't have time for this." Gina brushed past me and made her way toward the front of the guesthouse.

What a pleasant woman. No wonder she and Honey didn't get along. They were cut from the same cloth.

The front door slammed a second later, and I exhaled

slowly. I switched off my flashlight app but didn't walk off right away. I frowned at Richard's door. I hadn't known that Jessie went running with Gina. And I had never seen them go out at this time either—though, I hadn't exactly been up as early every morning this week. And if Gina had been here for Jessie, why had she been outside Richard's door?

Jessie hadn't mentioned she was friends with Gina either. But why would she? It had never come up in conversation.

I shook my head. I had to admit that not everything was related to the case. But it was suspicious that the wedding planner who definitely had a motive was in the guesthouse at this hour, and, apparently, hanging out with Jessie. I'd have to remember to ask Jessie about it later.

Right now, I needed to get out on the truck and start preparing it for the day.

We'd spent too much time worrying about the murder and too little serving food on the beachfront. Today would be the day we got back on track. I felt it in my bones. Or maybe that was the cold.

I stepped out and smiled at those hints of sunlight on the horizon. The street outside was shrouded in pre-dawn gray, and the wedding planner was nowhere to be seen.

"Come on, Ruby, focus," I murmured and headed for

the food truck, its candy pink and green stripes beckoning to me.

Fifteen

By eight, we were parked out on the beachfront with our display cases stacked full of delicious cupcakes and treats and two pots of coffee brewing behind us. One was decaf and the other normal espresso, a strong aromatic bean that filled the inside of the truck with the scent of a warm welcome to another morning in Carmel Springs.

Bee had prepared a spiced pumpkin puree with almond milk, and I'd chalked in pumpkin-spice lattes on the specials board on the back wall, as well as on the clapboard we placed next to the truck each morning.

If pumpkin-spice lattes didn't bring in the crowds, I didn't know what would.

"Hmm." Bee checked on another batch of cupcakes baking in the oven. "Hmm."

"What is it? The cupcakes aren't rising?"

Bee laughed. "No, of course they are. I was just thinking about what you told me."

"About Gina?" I asked, lowering my voice, though there was no one around to hear except for the wind, the seagulls, and the cold, gray ocean this morning.

"Exactly that. Interesting that she was in the guesthouse. Hovering around. Hmm."

"You think she might have been involved?" I asked.

"We can't be sure, but she definitely had a motive. But then, why would she have been snooping around the guesthouse?"

"She was standing in front of Richard's door." I had too many questions and no answers. We didn't know enough about Jessie or Gina to make any deductions just yet. "I think we need to do more research on those two if we're going to figure out who—"

Bee hissed as a figure came into view. And then another and another.

"What on earth?"

"It's Millie," Bee said, a smile parted her lips. "Millie and some friends. A lot of friends."

"Customers." I nearly shouted at the prospect.

Bee was just as ecstatic, though she hid it better than I did.

"Hello there, dears," Millie said, coming to a halt in

front of the truck's window. "I thought you two might have just what my associates and I need for breakfast."

"Your associates?" I asked.

"Yes," Millie said. "These are a few of the writers on our team at the paper. And Kevin over there is the food critic I told you about."

A stocky man wearing a thick, puffy black jacket waved at us. He was balding with a sharp nose, but he had kind eyes. Hopefully, he had kind fingers too. The last thing the truck needed was a bad review on top of everything else going on.

"Wonderful," I said. "Well, we're open for business. What would you like, Millie?"

"I'll have one of those pumpkin-spice lattes, please, and a vanilla-caramel cupcake."

"Absolutely," I said and flew into action.

We served the customers two at a time, doling out delicious treats, from the cupcakes to the mudslide minis we'd served the week before, to pieces of pumpkin pie Bee had made in anticipation of Thanksgiving, which was just around the corner.

I'd come up with the idea for a few spooky skeleton cupcakes for Halloween as well. Holidays, whether Halloween or Christmas or Thanksgiving, were my favorite days of the year.

The cupcakes nearly sold out, and the writers and the

food critic—my stomach did a turn and a dip at the sight of him tucking into his cake—went to sit on the benches overlooking the ocean. Millie hung back, sipping on her latte.

"This is delicious," Millie said.

"It was Bee's idea. You know, now that fall's here, pumpkin spice and everything nice is in order."

Millie set down her Styrofoam cup on the counter and peeled back the paper on her cupcake. She took a bite. "Oh wow. Oh my gosh. If Kevin doesn't give you a five-star review, I'm going to have to find another critic for the paper. Because this is just..."

"Thank you," I said. "It's all Bee. She's an amazing baker."

"Now, stop that, both of you." Bee flapped her hands at me. "Flattery doesn't fit me well. I think it's because I eat too many cakes."

"How could you not when they taste so good?"

Bee fanned her face, but it did nothing to banish the redness in her cheeks. "Well, thank you, anyway. I've been working on improving my craft. It's nice to know it's appreciated. And it's nice to finally serve some customers after all this time."

"Yes, thanks for that, Millie. Having people to serve is a blessing."

Millie finished off her cupcake and licked her fingers.

Others sat on their benches doing the same. "Judging by the reactions to your food, it looks like you'll have a few return customers," Millie said. "Word spreads fast in this town. I'm sure the other residents will get over themselves and come try your stuff, especially once these guys start telling them how amazing it is. I know I'll be doing the same."

"You're too nice, Millie."

"I'm always willing to help a woman out," she said. "Especially one who's running her own business. Heaven knows we need all the help we can get."

The whoop of a police siren cut across the last part of her sentence. The satisfaction that had come with serving customers evaporated instantly. It was Detective Jones. Again.

"If he's coming to shut down the truck, he's about to get more than just the keys," Bee said, rolling up her sleeves. "I took a jujutsu class last spring, and I'd be happy to give the man a lesson. And a black eye."

And I had a black belt in karate—not that it ever helped me with my panicky Beaning moments. That was an obstacle I had to overcome. "Bee, I don't think knocking out a police officer is going to curry much favor with, well, anyone in town."

"You'd be surprised," Millie whispered, lifting her cup

to cover her mouth. "Most people in town aren't exactly Jones's best friend."

"That seems to be a trend around here." Bee sniffed. "He's lucky he hasn't been murdered yet." She'd said it a little too loudly, and Detective Jones stopped a few steps from the truck, glaring at her.

"That you threatening a police officer, Miss Pine?"

"Take it how you want it," Bee replied. "Hobbit man."

The detective next to Jones—Martin, if I wasn't mistaken—snorted but passed it off as a sneeze. Hints of mirth danced at the corners of his lips.

He has a nice smile. Oof, I had to get it together. Detective Martin was probably my age, maybe a little younger even, and I was not interested in dating—particularly not a detective who may or may not think I was a murderer.

Jones sauntered up to the truck, his thick thumbs tucked into his belt loops. "I see you're back in business. Folks around here usually got their heads on straight. I wonder what changed." He cast a beady-eyed glare around. The diners ignored him.

Detective Martin tapped a display case. "Those look good. The vanilla-caramel cupcakes. Can I get one, please?"

Polite too. And he's got dark hair. I liked men with dark

hair. I also liked not having my heart broken. "Yes," I said stiffly and went to get one for him.

"What are you doing, Martin? You can't buy food from a person of interest."

"It's just a cupcake."

"And murder is just a felony."

"Good heavens, don't be so melodramatic, detective," Millie put in. "I mean, really, it's baked goods. And from what my sources have told me, you don't have anything solid on either of these ladies."

"Your sources are wrong," Jones snapped.

"That explains why you've arrested Bee and Ruby."

"Listen," Jones said, as I handed over a boxed cupcake to Martin, "I came out here to warn you old bats to stay out of trouble."

"Bats?" Bee asked and started removing her earrings. "You'd better get him out of here, Ruby, if you want to keep me out of jail."

"Word on the street is you two have been following people around," Jones said. "That's suspicious behavior. I hear one more thing like that, and your butts will be locked up faster than you can put extra weight on 'em from your cakes." He marched off back to the cruiser.

"Let me at 'em," Bee said, trying to sidestep me to get to the truck's door.

I blocked her path. "It's not worth it, Bee. Let him go."

I took a deep breath, but it didn't help dismiss the rage now bubbling through my veins. My hands shook as I rang up the cupcake order for Detective Martin. I held out his change.

"Keep it," he said, in a deep rumble. "Sorry about Jones." He opened his mouth as if he wanted to add something, but the moment passed, and he hurried off to join his partner instead.

We watched them leave, Bee with her fists clenched, Millie shaking her head, and me wiping down the counter to keep myself busy.

It was more important than ever that we get to the bottom of what had happened. If only to prove Jones wrong.

Sixteen

THE MOOD ON THE TRUCK HAD PICKED UP significantly after the run-in with the mean detective. Millie's friends and colleagues had, indeed, passed on the word about the truck's delicious treats, sweets, and coffees, and we'd been swamped with customers for the first time in more than a week.

We arrived back at the guesthouse just after four, starving, satisfied, and tired in the way only a hard day's work could bring.

"My feet are killing me," Bee said.

"Mine too." I dropped my handbag on the dressing table in my room. "But isn't it nice?"

"Definitely. A good change from all the vacation time we've been having. I only wish you hadn't stopped me from attacking that detective. As unwise as it is, he does deserve a good beating." Bee's lips had gone thin.

"Let's not worry about him now. Can you smell that?" The tempting scents of dinner being prepared drifted up the stairs and through my open bedroom door.

"I could eat a horse," Bee said.

I shut the door behind us, not even bothering to change out of the clothes I'd been wearing all day, and hurried downstairs. We took our usual spot next to the fireplace, relishing the warmth from the logs crackling in the grate.

The others hadn't come down to the tables, now separated and scattered throughout the living room. Their loss. Though, it would have been nice to catch up with Jessie, if just to ask her whether it was true that she and Gina were jogging buddies.

Samantha exited through the kitchen doors and spotted us at our table. "Good evening. Did you have a good day on your truck?"

"It was fantastic," I said.

"Apart from a brief incursion from the Lord of the Rings."

"That was Sauron, not Frodo."

"Fine, an incursion from the short, chunky, hairy, and mean guy."

"Detective Jones?" Sam asked.

"That's the one," Bee replied. "Although, he did have another detective with him too who was quite pleasing on the eye and the ear. Don't you think, Ruby?"

I shrugged. "He was fine."

"Fine like *fiiiiine*." Bee grinned at me.

"Oh, I know who you're talking about," Sam said. "That Detective Martin? He's new to Carmel Springs, but he seems like such a sweet guy. And, between us, he's the most eligible bachelor in town. Missi Lauren's mom told me that they're trying to get him to participate in the town's Halloween kissing booth this year."

"A Halloween kissing booth?" I asked. "Now I've heard everything."

"Interested, are you?" Bee nudged me. "He was giving you the eye."

I cleared my throat. "So, Sam, what's on the menu tonight? It smells amazing."

"I've made lobster mac 'n cheese," Sam replied. "I hope you're hungry. It's just come out of the oven with a freshly baked cheesy garlic bread."

"I have my suspicions that you're trying to make me fat." Bee leaned back and patted her belly. "I'm happy to report that it's been a resounding success so far."

"I'll be right back with your food," she said. "And some drinks? Milkshakes? Sodas?"

"A soda would be lovely."

"For me too," I said.

Sam hurried back into the kitchen, and the doors swung, brushing their ends against each other then settling. Trouble darted into the living room from the reception hall with a drawn-out *meoowww*. He rubbed against my ankles. The lobster had likely drawn him in.

"What was that about?"

"What?" I asked.

"I mentioned that handsome detective and you avoided the topic completely. Did I make you uncomfortable, Ruby?" Bee's hazel eyes had filled with concern.

"Oh. No. Not really. It's just..." How did I word this? I hadn't discussed this with anyone before, not even my work colleagues or my parents.

"It's fine," Bee said. "You don't have to tell me anything you don't want to."

I fiddled with the silverware. "My ex-fiancé left me a few years ago."

"I'm so sorry."

"He didn't just leave me, though. He ... well, he disappeared. I reported him missing and everything, but there were no leads, and from what I gathered from his parents, he's actually alive and well. But gone. He didn't even take his ring when he left. Daniel was supposed to be the love of my life."

Bee shook her head. "I don't know what to say."

"It's OK. It was tough at first. He worked at the paper with me, and when he disappeared, people who had been my friends started talking. They blamed me for his disappearance as if I had chased him away. He was a star journalist too. It was just so odd."

"That must be so difficult for you. It sounds like you had no closure."

I thought about that. "I guess you could say that this is my closure. Traveling around in the food truck. I don't want to settle down anywhere. I just want to keep moving and forget about all of that stuff."

The kitchen doors opened, and Sam emerged with a tray. On top of it, she'd positioned two steaming plates of lobster mac 'n cheese, garlic bread in a basket, and two sodas, bubbling in their glasses.

"Wow," I said, and the negativity that had come with mentioning Daniel's name disappeared. How could I possibly be sad about that when I had such great company and amazing food to eat? "Thank you so much, Sam."

"Absolutely. Let me know if you need anything else."

"Why don't you join us?" Bee asked. "It would be lovely to have the company."

"Are you sure?"

"Of course," we exclaimed, in unison. Trouble meowed his agreement.

Seventeen

"I'm going to roll into bed," Bee said, struggling up the stairs after dinner and a sumptuous caramel cheesecake for dessert. "I wasn't kidding about Sam's plans to fatten me up, you know. I've gained at least ten pounds today."

I laughed. "There are worse fates." My mirth was overwhelmed by a jaw-creaking yawn. I was exhausted, and the thought of curling up in my warm bed, perhaps even with little Trouble for company, was heaven.

The kitty cat chased up the stairs after us, batting at the shoelaces of my sneakers. We reached the landing and trooped across it. It took me a second to register that Trouble hadn't followed. The kitten hopped back and forth on the top step, his fur standing on end and back arched.

"What's wrong, Trubby?" I asked.

"Huh?"

"Look at the cat," I said. "He doesn't want to come up here."

Bee's mouth formed an 'o' shape. "I've heard about this. It's a spirit."

"What?"

"Cats can see ghosts. See? Look how he won't come any further up the stairs? There's a ghost blocking his path."

"Bee, that's..."

"Don't say ridiculous, Ruby, don't you dare. Anything's possible, you know." Bee shivered and rubbed her arms. "I wonder if it's Honey's spirit. I mean, they say that murder victims often don't know they've passed on. And they can't let go of their old lives. So they stick around and—"

A creaking noise drew my attention. Bee jumped on the spot.

I'd never have taken her for someone easily spooked. She usually ran toward danger. "Relax, Bee, it's just a creaking door or something. Why are you so jumpy?"

"It's just the thought of facing something I can't see."

"There's nothing here." But Trouble kept up the same odd behavior, hissing and hopping around, his glowing yellow eyes fixed on a spot nearby.

I followed his line of sight and gasped.

"What? What is it?" Bee grabbed hold of my arm.

"My door," I whispered. "It's open."

That was what the creaking had been. My bedroom door was ajar, the lights off inside the room.

"Oh." Bee let out a sigh of relief.

"Oh? Now you're relaxed?"

"Of course. Ghosts don't open doors."

"But murderers might," I whispered.

Was that what had spooked Trouble? A stranger in the guesthouse?

"We should call the police."

Bee nodded. "But our phones are in there."

"Right." I took a step forward and then another one back. "Right. So. Um. Maybe?"

"Come on, let's go in. It's two against one." Bee tucked her arm into mine and walked forward, guiding me along with her. Trouble hissed and gave a terrific kitty meow, but there was no stopping us now.

Bee opened the door. I reached in, feeling along the wall for the light switch.

"Aha!" Bee yelled, leaping into the room as the yellow light filled it to the corners. She lifted her hands and positioned them like a Kung-Fu master. "Come out, right now. We're armed, dangerous, and not afraid to take you down."

But silence greeted her. A gentle rush of wind parted the curtains.

"The window's open," I whispered, scanning the rest of the room. Everything looked in order, except for... "My purse." It had been tipped over, the insides spilling out across the side table and the wooden floor.

Bee hurried from the window. "Was anything taken?"

"I don't know. Let me check." I bent and sifted through my things.

"Careful not to touch any of it. There might be finger-prints the police could use. It might have been the murderer."

"I find that a far more chilling thought than the ghosts," I said.

"Forget ghosts. Ghosts don't need to open doors." Bee was so matter-of-fact that it would've been funny if not for the burglary. Or break-in. "I don't understand it," she continued, "why come in through the door and leave through the window? Or did they come through the window and sneak out through the door? Hmm." She strode back to the window and peered out. "There's nothing out there."

"Oh no," I said.

"What is it?"

"The keys to the food truck." The blood drained from my face and fingertips. "They're gone."

It had taken about an hour for Jones to get his butt from the police station down to the Oceanside Guesthouse, even though the guesthouse was probably a five-minute drive for the man.

He emerged from his cruiser and met us in front of the food truck, stamping his feet and shouting over his shoulder at Detective Martin. The handsome partner followed, settling his hat on his head.

"Good evening, ladies," he said.

"I don't handle break-ins." Jones glared at us. "You're wasting my time calling me out here. I'm in the middle of a murder investigation."

Bee growled under her breath.

I inhaled, trying to be the calm one in this situation. If we let Jones get to us too much, we'd end up getting in trouble for arguing with him. Unfortunately, he had the power in this scenario. There wasn't much we could do except what he wanted.

"Well?" Jones prompted. He folded his arms, and the light from the lampposts outside the guesthouse caught the half-circles of sweat under his arms.

It wasn't late yet, but exhaustion only heightened my irritability. "We have reason to believe that it might've been the murderer who broke in."

"This ought to be good," Jones muttered.

"You see," I said, cutting over the insult Bee had been about to lodge at the detective, "we witnessed someone in a mask and hood peering through the windows of the guesthouse. They dropped Honey's engagement ring, remember?"

"That's classified information."

"If the murderer believed we had the engagement ring, maybe they broke in to find it," I said.

"Pardon me, ma'am," Detective Martin said, tipping his hat toward me, "but on the call, you mentioned that your truck's keys had been stolen."

"Correct." At least he was polite. *And handsome.* Oh, I had to stop with that. It was pointless.

"Why would the murderer have wanted the truck's keys, ma'am? If they were after the engagement ring, that is."

I stalled, searching for the answer. But there wasn't one that made sense. He was right. Why on earth would the killer have taken the truck keys?

"Maybe, they thought we'd hidden the ring in the truck. They might not have known we handed it over to the police," Bee said, raising a finger.

"Or maybe," Jones said, "this is a waste of my time."

"It's not. Listen, detective, I know we haven't gotten

off to the best start, but you have to take this seriously. The murderer—"

"Is my business and not yours, little lady," he said. "Now, we're leaving. Another unit, one that's not actively investigating a murder, will come over to take your statements and help you out." He charged off again. The cruiser door slammed.

"Sorry," Detective Martin said, "I—uh. I'd better go." And he hurried off as well.

"That's just great." Bee tried the front door of the truck. "What are we supposed to do now?"

"Wait for the other cops, I guess. And call a locksmith to come out tomorrow and help us get the truck open."

"You don't have a spare set of keys?" Bee asked.

I blushed. "No, they were both on the key ring that was taken. Oops."

"Oops, indeed."

We waited on the steps of the Oceanside for the police to come over, and I contemplated what had happened, turning it this way and that, trying to make sense of it in my mind. If it hadn't been the killer, but someone who wanted to steal the truck then why hadn't they used the keys, started the truck and made off with it? They'd had their chance while we'd been at dinner.

If only I could figure out why they'd snatched the keys.

And who they were.

Eighteen

SUNLIGHT SLANTING ACROSS MY PILLOW WOKE me. I sat up, scrubbed the sleep from my eyes, and yawned. I lifted my filigree watch from the bedside table and checked the time. "What!" I bolted out of bed, upsetting Trouble, who had been napping near my feet. "What on earth? It's nine? Why didn't anyone wake me?"

I grabbed my robe from the back of the bathroom door and slipped it on. I rushed into the bathroom and to the door opposite that connected to Bee's room. I pounded on it.

"Easy, easy," Bee called out. "Some of us are trying to sleep in here."

"Bee, wake up! It's nine. The truck. We have to—"

The door cracked open, and Bee's bleary-eyed glare peered through at me. "Ruby, the truck's locked. Remember? And we can't get in? The locksmith's coming at ten. We've still got an hour to get ready."

The reality settled around me, and I let out a breath. "Oh. Right. I completely forgot."

"That's apparent," Bee said. "Now, if you don't mind, I'm going to grab myself a cup of coffee. Take your time in the bathroom." She snapped the door shut and shuffled off, humming under her breath.

I rubbed my eyes and caught my haggard reflection in the mirror. Good heavens, I needed a shower, a fresh set of clothes, and about twenty cups of coffee.

A shower and two cups of coffee later, I was more ready to tackle the day. I'd brushed my hair, slapped on some lip gloss and mascara, and missed one of Sam's delicious breakfasts, but we could always go grab something to eat after the locksmith had come.

It was just such a pity that we'd lost a day of work on the food truck when we'd been growing popular again.

At ten, I knocked on Bee's door, and we made our way down to the truck. I tried the door, but it was still locked up tight. Whoever had taken the keys had kept them and left the truck behind.

"How strange," I said. "Why wouldn't they steal it?"

"I find it odd, as well. Unless they wanted something inside it?"

"What if they stole our cupcake ingredients?"

"Or my recipe book!" Bee clenched her fists. "Hell hath no fury like a Bee who's had her recipes stolen."

"Catchy."

Bee smiled, but it soon faded to worry. "It doesn't look like it's been vandalized or anything. I don't understand. Why would they have done this? There's no reason to break into someone's room and steal something as useless as a set of keys without taking what they open."

"Exactly. Oh, here he is."

The locksmith arrived in a truck with his name along the side in snazzy print: *Guy's Locks and Car Keys.* He leaped out of the truck, spry despite his weight. His shirt lifted over his belly, and his jeans were barely held up by his belt. He smelled strongly of metal shavings.

"What we got here?" he asked, shaking my hand and then Bee's. "Missing keys?"

"Correct," I said. "We didn't want to break the window."

Guy sucked his teeth. "Good choice, ma'am. Good choice. Wouldn't want to cost yourself extra money. Give me a half-hour, and I'll have it all fixed for ya. New set of keys and everything."

We retreated to the Oceanside's front porch to watch, and Sam came out bearing two cups of coffee and a plate of cookies.

"I thought you might want these while you wait." Sam

seemed to droop as she handed them over. "I can't believe this has happened to you. And at my guesthouse again. What am I going to do about this? I always figured our town was safe. Obviously, there are always those petty theft cases, but this is getting out of hand."

"Sam, this isn't your fault," I said, taking a bite of a crumbly yet gooey chocolate chip cookie. "You've been a fantastic host."

"Exactly," Bee put in. "It feels more like we were the ones who brought all this negativity down on you rather than the other way around."

"Now you're starting to sound like Detective Jones."

Bee shot me a look over the rim of her coffee cup. "I've never been so severely insulted in my entire life, I'll have you know."

"Apologies. I was being overly dramatic."

"I'll accept it."

Sam sat down heavily on one of her porch chairs. "If word gets out that another break-in has happened here, I don't know what I'm going to do. No one will want to visit."

"Sam, please, don't worry about this. We'll find a way to make it better." But I had no idea how we'd do that.

I contemplated while Guy finished up. Soon, he came back to us with a fresh set of keys. "All done," he said, as he placed the keys in my palm. "Y'all give me a call if you need anything else."

"We will, thank you." I paid him, and once he was gone, Bee and I approached the truck. "Now, we get to see if anything's missing."

"My recipe book," Bee hissed.

I unlocked the truck with our new keys, and we piled inside. Bee made a beeline for her secret recipe book hiding spot in the corner cupboard and emerged with it in her hands. She clutched it to her chest, breathing heavily. "Thank goodness. My culinary secrets are safe."

"You know, the police should really be here. They should be taking fingerprints."

"Don't even get me started."

I went through the ingredients and checked the boxes, made my way from the back of the truck to the front, searching high and low in case the key thief had taken something or left evidence behind. I sat down in the driver's seat and something poked me where the sun didn't shine.

"Ow!"

"What is it? Are you all right?" Bee rushed through to the cab.

"I'm sitting on some—" I removed the object.

It was a glittery pink smartphone, the screen sleek black.

"I didn't know you upgraded," Bee said.

"I didn't," I replied. "This isn't mine."

"I'm not the glittery pink type."

"Then whose is it?" I unlocked the screen. There was no passcode. An image of Honey Wilson was the background. She wore her flesh-colored bikini and a pair of high heels. "It's Honey's phone," I said.

"Are you sure?"

I showed her the screen.

"What's it doing here?" I asked and opened up her messages. Just to be sure this was really her phone and not someone else's. I doubted William would have had a glittery phone, even with Honey's picture as a background.

"What's that?" Bee asked. "That message there?" My partner in baking leaned against my seat and tapped on the screen.

A message opened.

I told you you'd regret this. You should have just done what I wanted from the start. You're going to die today.

It was dated on the day of her murder. From a number that wasn't in her phone contacts. Bee and I stared at each other, wide-eyed. "Who? How? Why?"

"Yeah, my thoughts exactly," Bee said. "Quick, let's copy the number down. We have to report this to the police."

I blinked. "But..."

"The person who stole the truck keys must have planted the phone in here. They wanted to frame you as the murderer. In fact, I wouldn't be surprised if the cops pull up before we can even call them. We have to act quickly," Bee said, her own phone out of her pocket. She copied down the strange number then took the glittery phone from my hand and wiped it down. "We don't want them to have anything on you."

"I can't believe this is happening. Why?"

"I don't know," Bee said, as she put the phone in the glove box. "But we're going to find out."

Nineteen

"THAT MAN!" BEE STAMPED HER FOOT SO HARD she almost tripped. "I can't believe we have to endure dealing with him at all." She glared after the police cruiser.

It turned the corner at the end of the street. The pressure in my chest stayed the same. Detective Jones and his partner had rolled up and snatched the phone from us before we'd even called them. No amount of explaining what had happened seemed to make a difference.

From what Jones had said, he clearly believed that I'd had Honey's phone because I'd killed her and had wanted to hide the evidence from them. Patently untrue, of course.

"It's OK, Bee. We're going to figure this out on our own. You have the number, right?"

"Right," Bee said and removed her phone from her pocket.

We retreated to the porch—so we wouldn't look strange, standing in the middle of the road fiddling with a phone—and huddled together.

"Here we go. Let's see who answers," Bee said and hit dial. She turned up the volume and put it on speaker. The dial tone beeped and a voicemail message came through. "Shoot. No answer."

"Or it's off."

"Or maybe it was a burner phone. The killer used it and threw it away to ensure the police couldn't latch on to their signal."

"Personally, I wouldn't have been worried. I doubt Jones knows anything about triangulating a signal," I said.

Bee tried the number again but to no avail. There was simply no answer, and we were out of luck. Bee sighed and tucked her phone back into the pocket of her jeans. "I'm stumped," she said. "We know the wedding planner might have been up to something, but we have no real proof other than the fact that she might not have liked Honey."

"And there was the whole Richard-in-the-will deal." I chewed on the inside of my cheek. We definitely weren't going to be driving out to the beach today to serve our treats, and that meant we'd have some time to work on the case. "I have an idea."

"Shoot." Bee leaned against the railing. "I'm willing to try anything at this point."

"Well, there's one obvious avenue we haven't investigated yet. We could talk to William."

Bee pulled a face. "Only one problem with that. If we upset him, he's likely to go tell the detective about it."

"It's probably a chance we have to take, regardless."

"I agree. Let's do it." Bee's hazel eyes were aglow with excitement.

We bundled into the guesthouse and up the stairs to the second floor where William and Honey had been staying together. Over the past few days, we'd only seen William briefly, always in passing, and he'd looked tired and sad.

According to just about every crime show I'd watched, the significant other was usually the prime suspect in a murder case, but talking to William right after Honey's death had seemed like a crass thing to do.

I knocked on his door, my mouth drying up.

A beat passed. Bee shifted next to me.

The latch clacked and William opened the door. "Hello," he said. "Can I help you with something?"

"Hi, William," I said. "You don't know us very well, but we just wanted to offer our condolences for your loss." *And shamelessly use that as an excuse to squeeze you for more information.* What if he had done it? What if William had killed Honey in a rage? They had fought a lot, after all, and the engagement ring had been removed from her hand. Maybe he'd wanted to keep it afterward.

William nodded. "Thank you," he said. "As I understand it, Honey was planning on having you cater the wedding."

"That's correct," I said.

"Thanks for stopping by."

"Oh shoot," Bee said, "I almost forgot. I'll be right back." She rushed back down the stairs, leaving me alone with a potential murderer. Not that it was a problem or anything. *Wait, no, that's a huge problem.*

"If that's all?"

"Oh, I just, uh..."

Bee's footsteps hurried back and she reappeared, carrying a Bite-sized Bakery pink and green striped box. "Here," she said, pushing it into William's hands. "They're cupcakes for you to enjoy. Where I come from, it's customary to bring food to a wake. I know this isn't one, but..."

William clasped the box in his large hands, his usually handsome face crumbling slightly. His chin quivered. He took a deep breath. "Thank you. That's very kind. Please, come in. Have some coffee and one of these. I'm leaving soon. It would be nice to have some company while I pack."

Bee and I exchanged a glance and followed him into the room.

His was much larger than ours, with a four-poster bed decked out in white and teal cushions. He had an amazing view of the ocean, a balcony, and a pair of sofas. A flat-screen TV hung on the wall, and I spied a bathroom, tiled, with a four-footed Jacuzzi inside it. Good heavens, William had to be paying Sam an arm and a leg for this room.

"Please," he said, gesturing to one of the sofas.

Bee and I sat down. William set the cupcakes on the table in their box then prepared the coffee.

"I can do that," I said.

"No, it's fine," he replied. "I prefer to keep my hands busy. It's distracting." He fixed us coffee then came to take a seat. His bags were open on the bed, clothing folded neatly within, a pink makeup bag that had likely belonged to Honey on top of the pile. It was sad that William had kept that. Perhaps he missed her. That or he liked wearing makeup.

The ridiculous thought almost brought a smile to my lips, but I contained it. William wore a suit and a tie, his dark hair parted to one side—not exactly the makeup-wearing type.

"I'm sorry you haven't had much company," I said. "If we'd known, we would have made more of an effort."

"No, it's all right. In a way, I needed some time alone. I

had to process what happened." William shook his head. "I still miss her every day. I'm so sure I'll wake up one of these mornings and she'll be lying in bed next to me."

"Sorry." Bee was brisk about it. She reached for a cupcake and tucked into it, probably to keep herself from feeling too awkward about the whole thing.

"We spoke to Jessie," I said. "She was upset too. And Richard..."

"Richard handles things in his own way. We might look alike, but we're two completely different people." A slight tightening occurred around William's lips. He glanced off to one side. "Anyway, that doesn't matter. I'll be glad to leave this town."

"So, the police have told you you're allowed to go then?" Bee asked.

"Yeah," he said. "I have a rock-solid alibi. I hate saying that. I have an alibi for the morning of my fiancée's death." A bit of coffee spilled from his cup. "It's the worst thing I've ever had to say."

"Sorry," Bee and I said, in unison. It was easy to get into the habit, but I was sure that no amount of apologizing would make a difference to William.

"But Jessie's not leaving?" I asked.

"No, she's not." Again, a tightening around William's lips. "Not that she should. I'm not convinced that... No, never mind. Forget I said anything."

"Do you think she had something to do with this?" Bee asked. "If the police want her to stay, that might mean something."

William's tight lips drew even more so.

"She was upset about it, though," I said, trying to subconsciously nudge William toward the outburst that was so clearly on the way. "She was upset about poor Honey. Said that Honey had always been her friend and that it was such a shame she was gone."

"Is that what she said?" William's tone was ice.

"Pretty much verbatim," Bee put in.

"Evil little witch." The words came out hard, yet quiet. "She's nothing but a witch, that woman. She never wanted Honey and me to get married. She was always jealous of us. The day we got engaged and Honey posted a snap of her engagement ring online, Jessie had nothing nice to say about it."

"Oh."

"Yeah, she told Honey that I wasn't good enough for her. But Honey saw right through that. Truth is, Jessie's just jealous of us and always has been. She hates the fact that she married a man who's poor."

I didn't have words. It spoke to their characters that it mattered so much to them how wealthy their spouses were.

"Jessie and Honey were always competitive. And

Honey always won. Ever since I met her, they were at each other's throats, and I told the police as much, too. If anyone killed Honey, it was her." William set down his coffee to, I assumed, stop from spilling any more. "Jessie kept telling Honey what to do. She tried to give her legal advice, for Pete's sake, and all because she couldn't stand the fact that Honey was finally happy and doing better than her."

"Well," Bee said, "that's just terrible."

"Terrible," I echoed.

William sat back. "Anyway," he said. "I can't wait to be out of here. I thought coming back to my hometown would be refreshing and happy. I guess I was wrong. It's time for me to leave."

"We hope you feel better." I got up. "I know that probably won't be possible for a while."

"I'll be happy when that Jessie gets what's coming to her," William replied.

We let ourselves out of his room and walked down the hall in silence. The urgency to solve the case had peaked. Had Jessie done it? Had Richard? Clearly, William hadn't based on the air-tight alibi he mentioned. And there was still that wedding planner, Gina.

"What now?" I asked.

But Bee only shook her head.

Twenty

THE CORNER CAFÉ WAS LOCATED DIRECTLY across from the town hall in a brick building that claimed it was as old as the town itself. The pictures on the walls showed the first dirt road through the center of town, along with horse-drawn carriages and folks in old-timey clothes.

The atmosphere hummed with gossip and activity, and that was exactly the reason we'd come calling. If anyone would have seen something, it would be the people in this street. And servers were always eagle-eyed, looking out for new customers or for a chance to take a quick break from the grind of waiting tables all day.

Besides, this café smelled great, and we did need a break from walking, thinking, and deducing.

We took a table right in front of the window, and I

turned my gaze to the town hall. Its grand, dark doors were closed. Any evidence that a crime had been committed there was gone now—no police lines or cars or onlookers.

"Good afternoon! My name is Leon, and I'll be your server today." A teenager bobbed up and down next to the table, smiling. "Can I get you something to drink?"

"A coffee for me," I said.

"Pumpkin-spice latte, please."

Leon rushed off to put in the order.

"Here's how I see it," I said, once Leon had disappeared, leaning in so my words reached Bee's ears alone. "We've got three main suspects left. Jessie, Richard, and Gina. They all had reasons to get rid of her, though I think Richard's is probably the strongest with the whole will thing."

"True."

"Our problem is, we need to narrow down exactly who was at the crime scene on the day it happened. If they weren't there then they couldn't have done it."

Bee nodded. "The back door to that kitchen was rusted shut. None of the windows were broken. I have the pictures, and I'm positive there was no other way in."

"One entrance. The killer had to have used it." It was horrifying to think that the murderer might've passed us in the street after the deed. Or just missed us even. *What if we'd walked in on them in the act?* I grew faint at the thought.

Leon returned with our drinks, setting them down shakily. "Can I get you something to nibble on?"

"Sure," I said. "I'd like a slice of pie. Lemon meringue."

"Same for me. Say, Leon." Bee put her hand on his arm. "I wonder if you could tell us more about what happened at the town hall."

"The t-town hall?" he asked, tucking his pen and pad away. "You mean, the murder?" The last part came out as a whisper.

"That's exactly what I mean. I'm concerned," Bee said. "We're only here visiting, but it's scary to think that there might be a killer on the loose. Did you see who did it?"

"Oh no, no." Leon shook his head vehemently. "I didn't see anything like that. I mean, I didn't see anyone who looked like a killer. But I did notice there was kind of, like, a lot of activity over there. At the hall."

"Yeah? What kind of activity?"

"Oh, just people coming in and out." Leon turned to go, obviously done with the creepy conversation.

"What kind of people?" Bee asked.

He half-turned back, flinching under her intense gaze. "I don't know. People. Like a guy. I saw a guy go in there."

My heart pitter-pattered. "What did he look like?" I asked.

Leon shifted his weight from his right foot to his left. "He was tall. Dark hair."

"Did he have a mole?" Bee hissed.

"I don't know. I'll be right back with your food." Apparently, the question was just too much for Leon. He practically sprinted toward the front counter. It would have been amusing if I could think of anything other than what he'd told us.

Richard had definitely been there. Richard or William. But William had an alibi.

"Now, that *is* interesting," Bee said.

"You mean the fact that you scared that poor server out of his mind?"

"That too. But mostly that Richard was here. Of course, that doesn't rule out the other suspects. Just because Leon over there didn't see them doesn't mean they weren't here."

"Of course. But we can place Richard at the scene. That's a clue." Bee seemed satisfied, but I had my doubts.

Yes, Richard had a lot to gain, but my gut feeling said there was more to this than met the eye. But what was it?

Twenty-One

THE LEMON MERINGUE PIE FROM THE CORNER Café had been on the heavy side, but the walk down the beach, back toward the Oceanside, helped work off the calories. And got those investigative juices flowing.

Bee and I tossed ideas back and forth as we walked, our toes squidging in the cold sand. Our feet would be frozen by the time we got back to the guesthouse, but I couldn't bring myself to walk around with shoes on the beach.

"If only we had more information," I said.

"It's all circumstantial evidence," Bee agreed. "If we had something concrete, maybe we could make a citizen's arrest."

The thought drove a spike of panic through my stomach. *Relax. Nothing's going to happen.* "Do we really think it was Richard who did it?"

"The fact that he was there and that he had a motive to murder Honey points toward it. The changing of the will is a huge indicator that something was afoot."

But if it was Richard, why would he have brought so much attention to himself in the Chowder Hut the other night? He had confronted Jessie about her gossip session with Honey in front of everyone.

I stopped, facing the distant Oceanside, the dunes and scrubby bushes to my left and the ocean washing the sand on my right. "You know, Jones probably thinks we did it because of Honey's phone."

"Yeah, and Jones is also a—"

"No cussing, Bee."

"I wasn't going to, I swear. I was just going to point out that he has about as much investigative integrity as a rat with a crooked nose. That's all."

The wind whipped my hair back from my face and drove needles of cold against my skin. "We should probably..."

A lone figure had appeared on the path that led from the back of the guesthouse. Tall, with dark hair and wearing a trench coat that trailed through the sand. It was Richard! I grabbed Bee by the arm and dragged her behind some of the scraggly bushes, crouching low.

"What in the name of—?"

"Look! It's him."

Richard stopped once he'd reached the sand. He looked left and right then hurried off toward a line of bushes near the base of the embankment that led to the path above. He bent between the branches and rustled around, his coat flapping in the breeze.

"What on earth is he doing?" Bee whispered.

Finally, Richard straightened and ran his fingers through his hair. Once again, he appeared to check that the coast was clear then hurried back up toward the path that led to the guesthouse. I waited until he'd gone then piled out of our meager hiding spot.

Bee was practically dancing. "If that wasn't suspicious, then I don't know what is. This is it, Ruby. I can feel it in my baking bones."

We rushed over to the bushes. I reached into my pocket, removed my gloves and slipped them on. "Just in case," I said.

"Good thinking." Bee tapped her nose. "Don't want to contaminate the evidence."

I parted the bushes carefully. My jaw dropped.

Between them sat a hollow in the sand, carefully demarcated with stones, and filled with what could only be described as a treasure trove of junk.

"What is this?" I asked, shoving my way through to get a closer look.

"It looks like some sort of... nest. Except without bedding. And creepier."

I shifted some of the items aside. There were all sorts of things: a pocket radio, a watch on a long gold chain that appeared to have stopped working, a bottle of expensive bourbon, and a box that contained jewelry, both costume and real.

"He's a thief," I whispered.

"That would explain the whole financial difficulty situation and him being added into Honey's will."

A thought had occurred to me. Was it possible? It might just be the evidence we needed. Real proof that he had been the one to do it. "Got it!" I cried.

"What?"

I lifted a set of keys, dangling on the end of a donut keychain. "The keys to the food truck. It was him after all. He was the one who stole the keys. And he must have been the one who planted Honey's phone in the truck to try to frame us for the murder."

"Of course," Bee said. "Of course. He's been stealing because he needed money, and now that he's gotten it... well, he should be skipping town soon."

"We have to get this information to Jones." Though I didn't like the idea, Jones was the qualified professional here. He would have to be the one to take down Richard for the crime. Poor Honey. Likely, she'd trusted Richard. Why else would she have put him in her will?

"Stand back, Rubes," Bee said, "I've got to get some pictures of the scene. Put the keys back down, please. They're useless to us now, anyway."

I did as she asked then backed away from the pile of stolen goods. If we were right, and Richard was the killer, then why hadn't Jones arrested him? Unlike us, the detectives had access to actual evidence like fingerprints and perhaps other indicators we weren't aware of.

If they knew about the will and what Honey had included in it, and if they had questioned the others involved like Jessie and Gina, then why hadn't they made an arrest? It seemed so obvious.

I frowned.

But maybe it wasn't? No, no, this had to be it. It had to be Richard.

"All right," Bee said. "I think I've got everything I need."

"Let's get up to the guesthouse and make the call."

"We shouldn't leave the scene. The perp might return."

"The perp?"

"Perpetrator," Bee said.

"I know what it means. It's just funny that you're saying it." I giggled, but there wasn't any real mirth behind it. Richard had killed his brother's fiancée. That was an unimaginable crime, and it had been motivated by money.

The leads we'd pursued regarding Gina and the others had been for naught. Bee looped her arm through mine, and we hurried up to the guesthouse together, keeping an eye out for roving Richards in trench coats.

If it was him... But there were no more excuses. It had to be Richard. He wasn't even that likable of a guy, and he hadn't exactly been distraught over Honey's passing.

Then why does it feel like we're making a huge mistake?

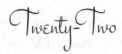

Twenty-Two

I ENTERED THE GUESTHOUSE THROUGH THE BACK door, searching the living room for any sign of the "perp." There was none. I gave Bee a thumbs-up over my shoulder. She immediately lifted her phone and made the call.

I slid the Oceanside's back door closed and kept guard, the hair on the back of my neck rising. We'd already confronted a killer once—well, two killers—and I didn't want to repeat the experience.

"—sad to see you go." It was Sam speaking from the front desk.

Curiosity nagged at me, and I crept forward, doing the *Pink Panther* walk without the music. I peeked around the side of the archway. William stood in front of the desk, his bags organized next to it and his card extended.

"I'm so sorry for your loss," Sam said, in her sweet

voice. "I wish it hadn't gone down like that. How is your family taking it?"

"Does it matter?" William asked.

His family. That's weird. Why didn't Richard and William stay with their parents while they were in town? And he'd just been terribly rude to Sam. He'd seemed quite sad when we'd spoken to him, apart from his rant about Jessie being the killer. What had changed?

"Oh. OK. Well, thank you so much for staying here."

"Yeah, whatever." William tucked his wallet into the pocket of his coat. He bent to lift his bag, and Trouble darted down the stairs. The kitten stopped at the sight of the ex-groom. His calico fur stood on end, his back arched, and he hopped back on the spot, hissing silently. "Your cat is weird."

"Oh, he's just, um..." But Sam couldn't manufacture an excuse, it seemed.

I grew hot all over. Something wasn't right here. I stepped out from my hiding spot and into the reception area. "Hello," I said, trying for a genuine smile. But I was too nervous, and even Samantha gave me an odd look. "Were you leaving, William?"

"Yeah," he said. "I need to get out of this town. It doesn't feel right to be here anymore."

"I can only imagine. Well, we'll miss having you around."

"Yes, we will," said Sam.

Once again, William was less than responsive to what Sam had said. Meanwhile, Trouble was still doing the hissing, hopping, and fur-on-end dance near the stairs. William lifted his bag and made for the door, and Trouble darted back upstairs, his tail thick.

I had to do something. William couldn't leave. *What's missing? Something isn't right.*

"Bee and I are calling the police, Sam," I said, loudly.

William stopped mid-stride, his hand on the doorknob. He didn't look back, but it didn't matter. He had stopped.

Think. Think, Ruby.

Trouble had reacted to William exactly the same as he'd done the night we'd found the keys missing from my room. Maybe it was that he'd smelled William's cologne? But it was proof enough for me. Hadn't Sam said that Trouble was a great judge of character?

"We think we've figured out who the murderer is," I said. "And the motive. The cops are on their way."

"Really?" Sam's hands flew to her mouth. "Who is it? Do I want to know?"

"Why don't you ask William?" It had been an impulsive thing to say and incredibly stupid too.

William spun around, dropping his bag. "What did you just say?"

"I said that Sam should ask you about who the murderer is."

Sam's head swiveled as she turned first toward William and then to me. "Um? What's going on?"

"I think William can tell you."

"I have no idea what you're talking about," William said, but already, he had started bearing down on me, a cool glint in his eyes, one he had hidden when I'd first met him and last spoken to him.

"It was easy for you, wasn't it? To pin it all on your brother?" It all made so much sense now. Honey hadn't wanted to marry William. William had tried to force Honey to put Richard in her will, as well, because that would pay off his brother and lay the blame on him too. Richard in the will when Richard didn't belong. "You're trying to frame your brother, aren't you?"

"It's none of your business, you nosy witch."

"I think it's everyone's business when there's a killer on the loose. What was it? The money?"

"Isn't it always the money?" William asked, cracking his knuckles. His usually handsome face transformed—anger twisted his lips and turned his eyes to slits. "I didn't even want to marry her. I didn't even love her."

"Well, your plan fell through," I said. "The cops are on their way."

"I don't believe you."

"It doesn't matter what you believe," I replied. The only thing that confused me was how William had an alibi. Unless...? Was his brother in on the whole thing? A flash of that pink makeup bag in William's suitcase came back to me.

I gasped. "You wore makeup. Of course. You faked a mole, and that's why you weren't seen. You pretended to be your brother." It was one thing to murder, but to frame his brother?

It was just so wrong.

"Yeah, you've figured it out," William said, waving his fingers like a magician. "Big deal. All that means is now I've got to kill you and that old broad too. If I didn't need Richard, he'd be a goner too, but he was so easy. Kleptomaniac kills woman for her money after being added to her will? The headline writes itself."

He swaggered toward me. "I had a feeling you two would cause me trouble. But I let it go because I figured, what harm could two women do? You're so busy baking your stupid treats you shouldn't have figured it out at all. And those cupcakes? They weren't even that good."

I opened my mouth to lambast him for the lie, almost offended more by the slight on Bee's cupcakes than I was by him murdering his fiancée and pinning it on his brother.

A terrific cry rose from the base of the stairs in the

hallway that led past the first floor rooms. Gina, the wedding planner, appeared out of nowhere. She let out another feral cry and launched herself across the room at William, a ball of fury and red hair.

He barely had time to turn. They crashed into the wall, fighting, her scratching and him trying to hold her off.

"What on earth?"

Sam screamed and ran out of the room. Bee appeared in the archway staring, wide-eyed. "What's going on?"

"It was William," I called. "He's the murderer. Are the police—?"

A siren whooped outside and two police cruisers skidded to a halt outside the guesthouse. It was over. Well, kind of. We'd still have to peel Gina off William for whatever reason.

Twenty-Three

"READ ALL ABOUT IT," MILLIE CRIED CHEERILY and slapped down the newspaper on the food truck's counter. "All the most important Carmel Springs news delivered directly to your eyes."

The ocean breeze ruffled the front page, and I grinned at Millie, lifting the paper up. "Thanks, Millie."

"Your review is in the food and recipe section," Millie said. "I think you'll like it, but then, you can probably tell it was positive, right?"

An entire row of customers stretched out behind her, waiting for their turn to order a coffee or a cupcake or another treat. Bee had baked up a storm all morning. It was only eleven, and we'd already sold out of our cupcakes once.

It was more than I could have asked for, especially after the past month we'd had in town.

"Thanks for this, Millie. It's great. I don't think the truck would have recovered without your help." It was like the universe had presented the bad, in William the murderer, and the good, in Millie who had selflessly helped us out with the truck and its consumer base problem. And the ugly? Well, Bee would have said that was Detective Jones, who'd successfully made the arrest.

"We did an article on the murder," Millie said. "My writer praised you and Bee for bringing the evidence to the police."

"Sure that went down well with Jones," Bee commented, as she served a customer and accepted their change.

"Oh, I saw him this morning. Let's just say he won't be buying another paper for a while." Millie grinned.

"You're an angel," Bee said. "A mudslide mini on the house for you."

"Can you believe the story with Gina Josephs?"

"Crazy," I said. "Absolutely crazy. Who would've thought that the wedding planner and the kleptomaniac were dating?" Apparently, Gina had been snooping around the guesthouse not because she went running with Jessie, but because she'd been involved with Richard.

Richard, who had been a total klepto, had no job. He

was who had actually stolen the ring and the truck keys from William's room after the murder. Apparently, he'd given Gina the ring. And Gina had dropped it outside the window when she'd been trying to spy on him from afar.

The Halloween mask? Well, that was a mystery to me.

Gina had been a bit of a head case but protective over Richard, hence her strange attack on William. Strange or not, it had saved my bacon. I could only be grateful for the subterfuge on her part. And now, William had been locked away for good, Richard had been arrested for minor theft, and Gina? Well, she'd gone back to LA but would probably be back to fetch Richard once he got out.

They were a match made in heaven.

"Just another week in Carmel Springs," Millie said and accepted her candy-striped box.

The next customer in line stepped forward and was served, and the rhythm continued, people wandering off with their boxes, some not able to stop themselves from eating before they'd made it two steps.

That was exactly how I'd always wanted it to be. The food truck overflowing with business, people enjoying the food, and us meeting interesting characters along the way. Although we'd had enough "interesting" to last us a lifetime.

After a long day on the truck, we arrived back at the guesthouse to find Sam outside, putting up Halloween decorations. Trouble danced around her feet, batting at a plastic skeleton leg, meowing and purring in between.

"Need any help?" I called. "I love Halloween."

"Oh, hello, ladies. I can use all the help I can get. I've got five new guests checking in for Halloween next week."

Bee and I hurried over to help her, and as we hung up spooky streamers and put out paper lanterns decorated in ghosts and bats and dancing skeletons, I couldn't help but feel that in a way, I'd found a place to call home. Even if it was temporary.

Catch more of Ruby and Bee's adventures in the Creepy Cake Murder, Book 3 in the Bite-sized Bakery Cozy Mystery series.

You can get it at any major retailer!

Craving More Cozy Mystery?

If you had fun with Ruby and Bee, you'll, love getting to know Charlie Mission and her butt-kicking grandmother, Georgina. You can read the first chapter of Charlie's story, _The Case of the Waffling Warrants_, below!

"Come in, Big G, come in." I spoke under my breath so that the flesh-colored microphone seated against my throat picked up my voice. "What is your status?"

My grandmother, Georgina—pet name Gamma, code name Big G—was out on a special operation. Reconnaissance at the newest guesthouse in our town, Gossip. The reason? First, she was an ex-spy, as was I, and second, the woman who'd opened the guesthouse was her mortal enemy and in direct competition with my grandmother's establishment, the Gossip Inn.

Who was this enemy, this bringer of potential financial doom?

A middle-aged woman with a penchant for wearing pashminas and annoying anyone who looked her way.

Jessie Belle-Blue.

It was rumored that even thinking the woman's name summoned a murder of crows.

"I repeat, Big G, what is your status?"

"I'm en route to the nest," my grandmother replied in my earpiece.

I let out a relieved sigh and exited my bedroom, heading downstairs to help with the breakfast service.

In the nine months since I had retired as a spy, life in Gossip had been normal. In the Gossip sense of the term. I'd expected that my job as a server, maid, and assistant would bring the usual level of "cat herding" inherent when working at the inn. Whether that involved tracking down runaway cats, literally, or providing a guest with a moist towelette after a fainting spell—tempers ran high in Gossip.

What was the reason for the craziness? Shoot, it had to be something in the water.

I took the main stairs two at a time and found my friend, the inn's chef, paging through her recipe book in the lime green kitchen. Lauren Harris wore her red hair in a French braid today, apron stretched over her pregnant belly.

"Morning," I said, "how are you today?"

"Madder than a fat cat on a diet." She slapped her recipe book closed and turned to me.

Uh oh. Looks like it's time for more cat herding.

"What's wrong?"

"My supplier is out of flour and sugar. Can you believe that?" Lauren huffed, smoothing her hands over her belly while the clock on the wall ticked away. Breakfast was in two hours and Lauren loved baking cupcakes as part of the meal.

"Do you have enough supplies to make cupcakes for this morning?"

"Yes. But just for today," Lauren replied. "The guests are going to love my new waffle cupcakes, and they'll be sore they can't get anymore after this batch is done. Why, I should go down there and wring Billy's neck for doing this to me. He knows I take an order of sugar and flour every week, and I get it at just above cost too. What's Georgina going to say?"

"Don't stress, Lauren," I said. "We'll figure it out."

"Right." She brightened a little. "I nearly forgot you're the one who "fixes" things around here." Lauren winked at me.

She was the only person in the entire town who knew that my grandmother and I had once been spies for the NSIB—the National Security Investigative Bureau. But the news that I had helped solve several murders had spread through town, and now, anybody and everybody with a problem would call me up asking for help. A lot of them offered me money. And I was selective about who I chose to help.

"I'll check it out for you if you'd like," I said. "The flour issue."

"Nah, that's OK. I'm sure Billy will get more stock this week. I'll lean on him until he squeals."

"Sounds like you've been picking up tips from Georgina."

Lauren giggled then returned to her super-secret recipe book—no one but she was allowed to touch it.

"What's on the menu this morning?" I asked.

Lauren was the boss in the kitchen—she told me what to do, and I followed her instructions precisely. If I did anything else, like trying to read the recipe for instance, the food would end up burned, missing ingredients or worse.

The only place I wasn't a "fixer" was in the Gossip Inn's kitchen.

"Bacon and eggs over easy, biscuits and gravy, waffle cupcakes and... oh, I can't make fresh baked bread, can I?"

"Tell her I'll bring some back with me from the

bakery." Gamma's voice startled me. Goodness, I'd forgotten about the earpiece—she could hear everything happening in the kitchen.

"I'll text Georgina and ask her to bring bread from the bakery."

"You're a lifesaver, Charlotte."

We set to work on the breakfast—it was 7:00 a.m. and we needed everything done within two hours—and fell into our easy rhythm of baking and cooking.

My grandmother entered the kitchen at around 8:30 a.m., dressed in a neat silk blouse and a pair of slacks rather than the black outfit she'd left in for her spy mission. Tall, willowy, and with neatly styled gray hair, Gamma had always reminded me of Helen Mirren playing the Queen.

"Good morning, ladies," she said, in her prim, British accent. "I bring bread and tidings."

"What did you find out?" I asked.

"No evidence of the supposed ghost tours," Gamma said.

We'd started hosting ghost tours at the inn recently, so of course Jessie Belle-Blue wanted to do the same. She was all about under-cutting us, but, thankfully, the Gossip Inn had a legacy and over 1,000 positive reviews on Trip-Advisor.

Breakfast time arrived, and the guests filled the quaint dining area with its glossy tables, creaking wooden floors, and egg yolk yellow walls. Chatter and laughter leaked through the swinging kitchen doors with their porthole windows.

"That's my cue," I said, dusting off my apron, and heading out into the dining room.

I picked up a pot of coffee from the sideboard where we kept the drinks station and started my rounds.

Most of the guests had gathered around a center table in the dining room, and bursts of laughter came from the group, accompanied by the occasional shout.

I elbowed my way past a couple of guests—nobody could accuse me of having great people skills—apologizing along the way until I reached the table. The last time something like this had happened, a murder had followed shortly afterward.

Not this time. No way.

"—the last thing she'd ever hear!" The woman seated at the table, drawing the attention, was vaguely familiar. She wore her dark hair in luscious curls, and tossed it as she spoke, looking down her upturned nose at the people around the table.

"What happened then, Mandy?" Another woman asked, her hands clasped together in front of her stomach.

Mandy? Wait a second, isn't this Mandy Gilmore?

Gamma had mentioned her once before—Mandy was

a massive gossip in town. Why wasn't she staying at her house?

"What happened? Well, she ran off with her tail between her legs, of course. She'll soon learn not to cross me. Heaven knows, I always repay my debts."

"What, like a Lannister from *Game of Thrones*?" That had come from a taller woman with ginger curls.

"Shut up, Opal," Mandy replied. "You have no idea what we're talking about, and even if you did, you wouldn't have the intelligence to comprehend it."

The crowd let out various 'oofs' in response to that. The woman next to me clapped her hand over her mouth.

"You're all talk, Gilmore." Opal lifted a hand and yammered it at the other woman. "You act like you're a threat, but we know the truth around here."

"The truth?" Mandy leaned in, pressing her hands flat onto the tabletop, the crystal vase in the center rattling. "And what's that, Opal, darling? I'd love to hear it."

"That you're a failure. You sold your house, left Gossip with your head in the clouds, told everyone you were going to become a successful businesswoman, and now you're back. Back to scrape together the pieces of the life you have left."

"Witch!" Mandy scraped her chair back.

"All right, all right," I said, setting down the coffee pot

on the table. "That's enough, ladies. Everyone head back to their tables before things get out of hand."

Both Opal and Mandy stared daggers at me.

I flashed them both smiles. "We wouldn't want to ruin breakfast, would we? Lauren's prepared waffle cupcakes."

That distracted them. "Waffle cupcakes?" Opal's brow wrinkled. "How's that going to work?"

"Let's talk about it at your table." I grabbed my coffee pot and walked her away from Mandy. The crowd slowly dispersed, people muttering regret at having missed out on a show. The Gossip Inn was popular for its constant conflict.

If the rumors didn't start here then they weren't worth repeating. That was the mantra, anyway.

I seated Opal at her table, and she pursed her lips at me. "You shouldn't have interrupted. That woman needs a piece of my mind."

"We prefer peace of mind at the inn." I put up another of my best smiles.

Compared to what I'd been through in the past— hiding out from my rogue spy ex-husband and eventually helping put him behind bars when he found me—dealing with the guests was a cakewalk.

"What brings you to Gossip, Opal?" I asked.

"I live here," she replied, waspishly. "I'm staying here while they're fumigating my house. Roaches."

"Ah." I struggled not to grimace. Thankfully, my cell phone buzzed in the front pocket of my apron and distracted me. "Coffee?"

"I don't take caffeine." And she said it like I'd offered her an illegal substance too.

"Call me if you need anything." I hurried off before she could make good on that promise, bringing my phone out of my pocket.

I left the coffee pot on the sideboard, moving into the Gossip Inn's spacious foyer, the chandelier overhead off, but catching light in glimmers. The tables lining the hall were filled with trinkets from the days when the inn had been a museum—an eclectic collection of bits and bobs.

"This is Charlotte Smith," I answered the call—I would never get to use my true last name, Mission, again, but it was safer this way.

"Hello, Charlotte." A soft, rasping voice. "I've been trying to get through to you. I'm desperate."

"Who is this?"

"My name is Tina Rogers, and I need your help."

"My help."

"Yes," she said. "I understand that you have a certain set of skills. That you fix people's problems?"

"I do. But it depends on the problem and the price." I didn't have a set fee for helping people, but if it drew me away from the inn for long, I had to charge. I was technically a consultant now. Sort of like a P.I. without the fedora and coffee-stained shirt.

"My mother will handle your fee," Tina said. "I've asked her to text you about it, but I... I don't have long to talk. They're going to pull me off the phone soon."

"Who?"

"The police," she replied. "I'm calling you from the holding cell at the Gossip Police Station. I've been arrested on false charges, and I need you to help me prove my innocence."

"Miss Rogers, it's probably a better idea to invest in a lawyer." But I was tempted. It had been a long time since I'd felt useful.

"No! I'm not going to a lawyer. I'm going to make these idiots pay for ever having arrested me."

I took a breath. "OK. Before I accept your... case, I'll need to know what happened. You'll need to tell me everything." I glanced through the open doorway that led into the dining room. No one looked unhappy about the lack of service yet.

"I can't tell you everything now. I don't have much time."

"So give me the *CliffsNotes*."

"I was arrested for breaking into and vandalizing Josie Carlson's bakery, The Little Cake Shop. Apparently, they found my glove there—it was specially embroidered, you see—but it's not mine because—" The line went dead.

"Hello? Miss Rogers?" I pulled the cellphone away from my ear and frowned at the screen. "Darn."

My interest was piqued. A mystery case about a break-in that involved the local bakery? Which just so happened to be run by one of my least favorite people in Gossip?

And when I'd just started getting bored with the push and pull of everyday life at the inn?

Count me in.

Want to read more? You can grab **the first book** in *the Gossip Cozy Mystery series* on all major retailers.

Happy reading, friend!

Made in the USA
Monee, IL
28 June 2025

20174560R00100

LIFE SCIENCE

ANIMALS HELP PLANTS

by Mary Lindeen

NORWOOD HOUSE PRESS

DEAR CAREGIVER, The *Beginning to Read—Read and Discover Science* books provide young readers the opportunity to learn about scientific concepts while simultaneously building early reading skills. Each title corresponds to three of the key domains within the Next Generation Science Standards (NGSS): physical sciences, life sciences, and earth and space sciences.

The NGSS include standards that are comprised of three dimensions: Cross-cutting Concepts, Science and Engineering Practices, and Disciplinary Core Ideas. The texts within the *Read and Discover Science* series focus primarily upon the Disciplinary Core Ideas and Cross-cutting Concepts—helping readers view their world through a scientific lens. They pique a young reader's curiosity and encourage them to inquire and explore. The Connecting Concepts section at the back of each book offers resources to continue that exploration. The reinforcement activities at the back of the book support Science and Engineering Practices—to understand how scientists investigate phenomena in that world.

These easy-to-read informational texts make the scientific concepts accessible to young readers and prompt them to consider the role of science in their world. On one hand, these titles can develop background knowledge for exploring new topics. Alternately, they can be used to investigate, explain, and expand the findings of one's own inquiry. As you read with your child, encourage her or him to "observe"—taking notice of the images and information to formulate both questions and responses about what, how, and why something is happening.

Above all, the most important part of the reading experience is to have fun and enjoy it!

Sincerely,

Shannon Cannon

Shannon Cannon, Ph.D.
Literacy Consultant

Norwood House Press • P.O. Box 316598 • Chicago, Illinois 60631
For more information about Norwood House Press please visit our website at www.norwoodhousepress.com or call 866-565-2900.
© 2019 Norwood House Press. Beginning-to-Read™ is a trademark of Norwood House Press. All rights reserved. No part of this book may be reproduced or utilized in any form or by any means without written permission from the publisher.

Editor: Judy Kentor Schmauss
Designer: Lindaanne Donohoe

Photo Credits:
All photos by Shutterstock

Library of Congress Cataloging-in-Publication Data
Names: Lindeen, Mary, author.
Title: Animals help plants / by Mary Lindeen.
Description: Chicago, IL : Norwood House Press, [2018] I Series: A beginning to read book I Audience: K to Grade 3.
Identifiers: LCCN 2018004459 (print) I LCCN 2018013273 (ebook) I ISBN 9781684041589 (eBook) I ISBN 9781599539027 (library edition : alk. paper)
Subjects: LCSH: Animal-plant relationships-Juvenile literature. I Pollination by animals-Juvenile literature. I Seed dispersal by animals-Juvenile literature.
Classification: LCC QH549.5 (ebook) I LCC QH549.5 .L56 2018 (print) I DDC 577.8-dc23
LC record available at https://lccn.loc.gov/2018004459

Hardcover ISBN: 978-1-59953-902-7   Paperback ISBN: 978-1-68404-149-7

312N-072018
Manufactured in the United States of America in North Mankato, Minnesota.

Look at the seeds!
They are blowing in the wind.
New flowers will grow
where the seeds land.

This big seed is floating
in the water.

A new tree will
grow where the
seed lands.

4

Wind and water help new plants grow.

They move seeds to new places.

Animals help, too.

Some seeds catch on fur and feathers.

Animals give these seeds a ride to a new place to grow.

Some seeds are inside of fruit.

Animals move these seeds
by eating the fruit.

Some seeds are inside of nuts.

Some animals hide nuts in order
to eat them later.

But not all hidden nuts get eaten.

Some grow into plants.

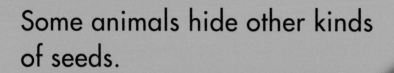

Some animals hide other kinds of seeds.

Some of these uneaten seeds will grow into new plants.

Animals also help new plants grow by walking on seeds.

They push the seeds into the dirt.

Then the seeds can grow.

Some plants can only make seeds if their flowers have been pollinated.

Animals help pollinate plants.

Did You Know?

Honeybees pollinate more flowers than any other insect.

Pollen sticks to an animal
when it touches a flower.

The pollen rubs off on other flowers the animal touches.

Lots of animals help
move pollen—

including people!

People also move seeds.

And they push seeds into
the dirt, too.

How can **you** help a new plant grow?

Animals Move Seeds

Animals Move Pollen

CONNECTING CONCEPTS

UNDERSTANDING SCIENCE CONCEPTS

To check your child's understanding of the information in this book, recreate the following graphic organizer on a sheet of paper. Help your child complete the organizer by identifying the main idea of this book and several details that tell about the main idea.

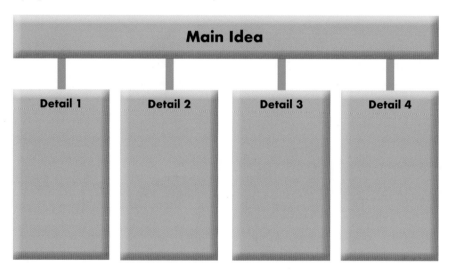

SCIENCE IN THE REAL WORLD

Using colored chalk, draw a flower on a sheet of paper. Then rub a cotton ball over the flower and look at the cotton ball. Chalk from the flower rubs off onto the cotton ball just like pollen from a flower rubs off onto honeybees and other animals.

SCIENCE AND ACADEMIC LANGUAGE

Make sure your child understands the meaning of the following words:

floating   hidden   insect   pollen   pollinate   uneaten

Have him or her use the words in a sentence.

FLUENCY

Help your child practice fluency by using one or more of the following activities:

1. Reread the book to your child at least two times while he or she uses a finger to track each word as it is read.

2. Read a line of the book, then reread it as your child reads along with you.

3. Ask your child to go back through the book and read the words he or she knows.

4. Have your child practice reading the book several times to improve accuracy, rate, and expression.

FOR FURTHER INFORMATION

Books:

Boothroyd, Jennifer. *Animal Pollinators*. Minneapolis, MN: Lerner Publishing Group, 2015.

Macken, Joanne Early. *Flip, Float, Fly: Seeds on the Move*. New York, NY: Holiday House, 2008.

Rice, Dona Herweck. *Pollination*. Huntington Beach, CA: Teacher Created Materials, 2014.

Websites:

National Geographic Kids: The Life Cycle of Flowering Plants
https://www.natgeokids.com/za/discover/science/nature/the-life-cycle-of-flowering-plants/

PBS Kids: Seed Racer
http://pbskids.org/plumlanding/games/seed_racer/

PBS Kids: Wild Kratts: Go Nuts
http://pbskids.org/wildkratts/games/go-nuts/

Word List

Animals Help Plants uses the 97 words listed below. *High-frequency words* are those words that are used most often in the English language. They are sometimes referred to as sight words because children need to learn to recognize them automatically when they read. *Content words* are any words specific to a particular topic. Regular practice reading these words will enhance your child's ability to read with greater fluency and comprehension.

High-Frequency Words

a	but	in	off	their	water
all	by	into	on	them	we
also	can	is	only	then	when
an	eat(ing)	it	other	these	where
and	get	look	people	they	will
any	give	make	place(s)	things	you
are	have	more	put	this	
at	help	new	some	to	
been	how	not	than	too	
big	if	of	the	two	

Content Words

animal(s)	floating	hide	later	pollen	sticks
blowing	flower(s)	honeybees	living	pollinate(d)	touches
catch	fruit	including	lots	push	tree
definitely	fur	insect	move	ride	uneaten
dirt	groups	inside	nuts	rubs	walking
eaten	grow	kind(s)	order	scientists	wind
feathers	hidden	land(s)	plant(s)	seed(s)	

About the Author

Mary Lindeen is a writer, editor, parent, and former elementary school teacher. She has written more than 100 books for children and edited many more. She specializes in early literacy instruction and books for young readers, especially nonfiction.

About the Advisor

Dr. Shannon Cannon is an elementary school teacher in Sacramento, California. She has served as a teacher educator in the School of Education at UC Davis, where she also earned her Ph.D. in Language, Literacy, and Culture. As a member of the clinical faculty, she supervised pre-service teachers and taught elementary methods courses in reading, effective teaching, and teacher action research.